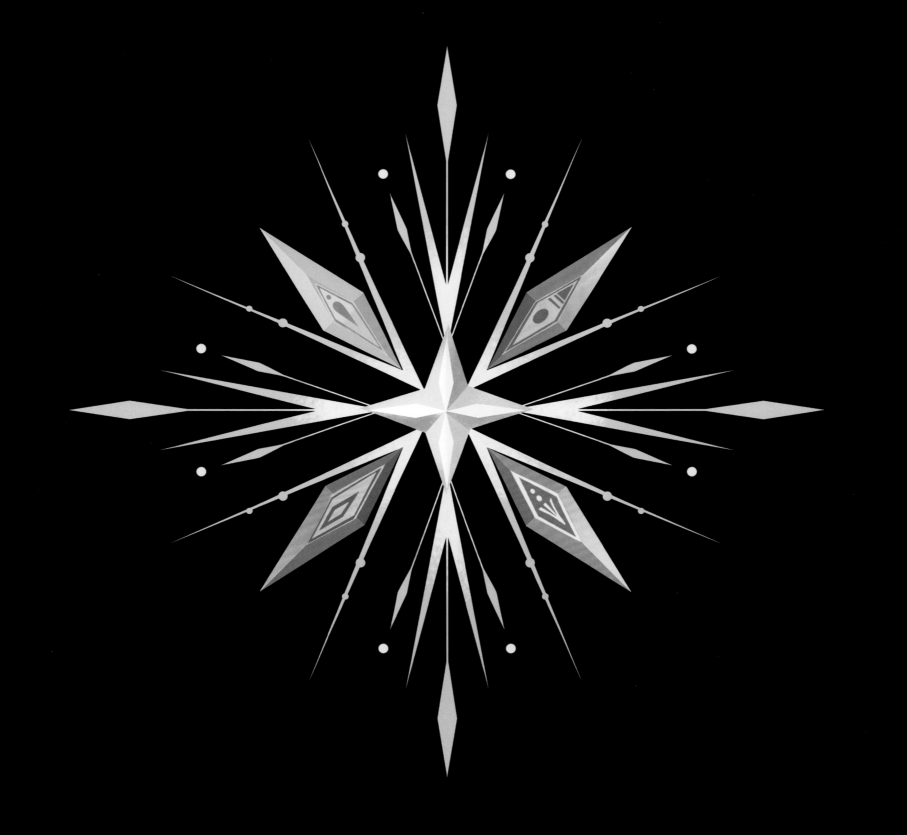

CHRONICLE BOOKS
SAN FRANCISCO

THE ART OF

Disney

FROZEN II

BY JESSICA JULIUS

FOREWORD BY CHRIS BUCK, JENNIFER LEE & PETER DEL VECHO

Creating a computer-generated animated film involves years of inspired collaboration.
Before the final rendered images of *Frozen 2* were seen on screens around the world,
the following artists contributed their talents to the images included in this book:

Alberto Abril, Alexander Alvarado, Chris Anderson, Iker de los Mozos Anton,
Virgilio John Aquino, Cameron Black, Ramya Chidanand, Johann Francois
Coetzee, Trent Correy, Charles Cunningham-Scott, Jennifer R. Downs, Colin
Eckart, Erik Eulen, Christopher Evart, Joshua Fry, Frank Hanner, Jay V. Jackson,
John Kahwaty, Hans-Joerg Keim, Si-Hyung Kim, Kate Kirby-O'Connell, Brandon
Lawless, Hyun Min Lee, Suki Lee, Richard E. Lehmann, Hubert Leo, Vicky
Yutzu Lin, Chris McKane, Terry Moews, Rick Moore, Nikki Mull, Michael
Anthony Navarro, Derek Nelson, Zack Petroc, Joseph Piercy, Svetla Radivoeva,
Liza Rhea, Jason Robinson, Brian Scott, Samy Segura, Rattanin Sirinaruemarn,
Justin Sklar, Jennifer Stratton, Lance Nathan Summers, Chad Stubblefield,
Marc Thyng, Timmy Tompkins, Mary Twohig, Wayne Unten, Jose Velasquez,
Elizabeth Willy, Michael Woodside, Alena Wooten, Walt Yoder, Xinmin Zhao

Library of Congress Cataloging-in-Publication Data
Names: Julius, Jessica, author.
Title: The art of Frozen 2 / by Jessica Julius ; foreword by Chris Buck,
    Jennifer Lee & Peter Del Vecho.
Description: San Francisco, CA : Chronicle Books LLC, [2019]
Identifiers: LCCN 2019010794 (print) |
    LCCN 2019013979 (ebook) | ISBN 9781452169873 |
    ISBN 9781452169491 (hardcover : alk. paper)
Subjects: LCSH: Frozen II (Motion picture) | Walt Disney Company. |
    Animated films--United States.
Classification: LCC NC1766.U53 (ebook) |
    LCC NC1766.U53 F585 2019 (print) | DDC 791.43/340973--dc23
LC record available at https://lccn.loc.gov/2019010794

Designed by Toby Yoo / t42design.

Manufactured in China.

MIX
Paper from
responsible sources
FSC
www.fsc.org
FSC™ C008047

10 9 8 7 6 5 4 3 2 1

Chronicle Books LLC
680 Second Street
San Francisco, California 94107
www.chroniclebooks.com

Front Cover: JUSTIN CRAM AND BRITTNEY LEE *Digital*
Back Cover and Endpapers: JUSTIN CRAM *Digital*
Case and Page 1: BRITTNEY LEE *Digital*
Pages 2–3: JAMES FINCH *Digital*

CONTENTS

FOREWORD

After *Frozen* was released, our thoughts began to turn to ideas for our next film. What new themes and worlds and characters did we want to explore? But as we heard from people all over the world about the impact *Frozen* had on them, we realized we weren't finished with Anna's and Elsa's story just yet. The idea that love is stronger than fear resonated more than ever, and we knew a sequel would have to be just as meaningful as the first film had been. It would have to be bigger and more epic, and the story would have to go even deeper. As we began to think about what was next for Anna, Elsa, Kristoff, Sven, and Olaf, we kept coming back to one weighty question: Why does Elsa have powers?

Elsa is now the queen of Arendelle, and she doesn't have to hide who she is anymore. She can be fully herself. But that raises a lot of questions. What does being queen mean to her? What would her parents think of her now? Is there a reason she has these magnificent ice powers? And what about Anna? What is she meant to do with her life? We started answering these questions by doing a ton of research, speaking with psychologists and trauma specialists, and diving deep into character assessments and personality tests. We began to uncover new layers to these characters, discovering that Elsa has many of the characteristics of a "protector," while Anna embodies the qualities of a "leader." That helped give us a road map showing where these sisters could end up in the next chapter of their story.

The first film was about Anna and Elsa wanting to be together, and they were finally reunited. But that doesn't mean they have to live in the same place together forever. Like all of us, they have to follow their own paths toward fulfillment and purpose. These personal journeys don't fundamentally change their connection with each other; they're still family. But in the second film they learn that they can live their own lives and still have confidence that the strong bond of love between them will never be broken.

As we dug into our character research, we also realized that Elsa and Anna would have a lot of unresolved issues with their parents. Like many young adults, they struggle to understand the choices their parents made, and they may need to forgive their parents for doing some things that they don't agree with. And because both parents were lost at sea, there are questions Anna and Elsa can't get answers to. A huge part of their journey in this film is figuring out how to move forward and find peace within themselves in order to become who they're meant to be.

As we developed *Frozen 2*, we learned more about the difference between myths and fairy tales, and understanding that distinction was a big turning point for us. Myths are about magical characters in an ordinary setting, beings who must bear the weight of the world on their shoulders and usually meet a tragic end. Fairy tales, on the other hand, are about ordinary characters in a magical world, people who must go through a difficult time but come out changed and triumphant. Myths are about hard truths. Fairy tales are about potential. Learning this was a lightning bolt of understanding: We realized that *Frozen* was a myth and a fairy tale running side by side! Elsa is a classic mythic character, while Anna is a classic fairy-tale character. *Frozen* would have been a very dark, mythic tragedy for Elsa if it weren't for Anna's fairy tale saving the day. Once we figured that out, we knew we couldn't stray from that structure in *Frozen 2*—that's their journey.

JUSTIN CRAM *Digital*

Elsa's magic is a central concern of *Frozen 2*, so we began to explore what it could mean. People believe in magic all over the world, but we wanted to know more about the magic of Old Norse and the cultures in Scandinavia, the region that helped inspire the world of *Frozen*. We started our research in books, learning about old sagas, legends, and folktales, and spoke with folklore experts, anthropologists, and linguists. That research informed our trip to Norway, Finland, and Iceland, where we met many people and walked the various landscapes, experiencing the sense of magic and spirit in each location. We wanted to connect Anna and Elsa to that feeling. We doodled a map of the fictional world of *Frozen*, with Arendelle at the bottom and a forested region farther north, bordered by a vast glacier. It made us wonder: What if these areas used to be united but are now broken lands? And what if Anna's and Elsa's mother is from the northern forests and is connected to its peoples who, for millennia, have conceived of magic as simply part of nature? Within that framework, Elsa's own magic began to make sense. Her magic takes the form of ice; it comes from water, one of the most fundamental elements of life. She's part of nature in an essential way. The whole story of *Frozen 2* opened up from there.

While Elsa is the only magical human in the *Frozen* world, we wanted to evoke the sense that nature itself is magical there. As humans we often take it for granted, but there are so many "magical" things that happen all around us, like leaves turning colors in the fall. We loved the idea of invoking that natural magic, particularly because it reminded us a little of how nature was alive in the Hans Christian Andersen fairy tale "The Snow Queen," which was the original inspiration for *Frozen*.

Frozen 2 is really a continuation of the first film; it's all part of the same story. We started this sequel with some trepidation because the expectations were tremendous, and we didn't want to let people down. But as the film began to take shape, it became its own entity, and we became less nervous about whether it would be as good as the first one; we just got excited about what it is. We stayed true to the characters and are following them on the next chapter of their story. We hope you'll love their journeys as much as we do.

—Chris Buck, Jennifer Lee & Peter Del Vecho

INTRODUCTION

In *Frozen 2*, Elsa, Anna, and Kristoff are becoming adults and trying to find their places in the world. They're maturing and growing emotionally, and they're journeying to places beyond Arendelle. Those changes are part of the narrative of *Frozen 2* and are reflected in its production design as well. The environments, costumes, and overall look of the film are more sophisticated and less innocent.

In both story and art direction, the filmmakers were inspired by the environments of Norway, Finland, and Iceland. "Trekking through forests in Norway and Finland felt like walking through a fairy tale. We could see why stories exist about 'hidden folk' living there. It felt enchanted, and very much Anna's world. Whereas Iceland, with its epic landscapes, was clearly a place where nature was in power. That was Elsa's mythic milieu," says production designer Michael Giaimo. "Much of the art direction was influenced by our time in those places."

The filmmakers wanted to depict a different season than in the first film and knew from the beginning it should be autumn. "Partly this was for the design aesthetic, since the color palette of autumn is so wonderful and rich," says Chris Buck, director. "But it also reflects the narrative. Spring is rebirth and summer is youth, but autumn is the maturing of the year, and these characters are maturing." The change of season proved to be quite a design challenge, says co-production designer Lisa Keene: "Autumn requires a whole new color palette that we had to define. And there's a lot more vegetation in the fall than in the winter." Adds Giaimo: "In autumn the colors are so strong and vibrant that the environment pulls attention from the characters and can make the performances hard to read. The *Frozen* color palette is strong, but there's a lot of subtlety too, and we wanted to bring

that aesthetic to this new palette. We warmed up the overall look of the film with fall colors like oranges and red-violets, especially in the vegetation and foliage, while bringing in the palette from the first film through the use of cooler and more neutral tones in the skies and deeper space. The warm foliage against a cool ambient environment gives *Frozen 2* a very specific look, which we hope audiences will recognize as distinct and unique to this film."

Though it was important to establish a new look for *Frozen 2*, sequels must also follow the established design rules for the world and characters, and maintain the visual style and sensibility of the first film. "That made visual development easier in some ways since we weren't starting from scratch," says Bill Schwab, art director of characters, "but it also created challenges because we had to make sure that all the new characters and environments look like they belong in the *Frozen* world. And because technology has changed significantly since *Frozen* in terms of how we build and render our characters, we actually had to completely rebuild Anna, Elsa, Kristoff, Sven, and Olaf, and adjust some of the designs."

Many of the design principles of *Frozen* are carried over into *Frozen 2*, including the use of verticals in character design, architecture, and environments, and intricate decorative pieces contained within defined spaces. "We tend to elongate and stretch all the elements, rather than have them run horizontal and squat. And they're not what we fondly call 'wonky'—we might cant an angle, but we don't offset and wiggle the lines. The overall aesthetic is very structured, long and elegant like Elsa," says Keene. One significant change is in the physical surroundings of *Frozen 2*. "For most of *Frozen*, almost everything was covered with ice and snow so you didn't see much of the ground. But in this film, we had to depict and then design what's actually underneath all that snow: leaves, trees, rocks, all kinds of natural objects and vegetation," says David Womersley, art director of environments.

The design team was inspired by classic Disney artists like Eyvind Earle and Mary Blair. Earle, says Giaimo, "had such a strong approach to design structure, and his work is so elegant. Both he and Blair used color theory and experimentation in very bold ways." The team also referenced fine artists such as Rousseau and Toulouse-Lautrec, as well as Norwegian illustrator Gerhard Munthe, German-American painter Albert Bierstadt, and several Russian painters who depict forests in all types of weather. "We create designs in our own manner, but the inspiration from these artists provides the underpinnings," says Giaimo.

The visual development team approached *Frozen 2* as a continuation of the design story, creating an original look while also bringing back elements from the first film in ways that add up to something new. Says Giaimo: "We hope the palette and production design in *Frozen 2* will surprise and enchant audiences all over again."

THE ELEMENTS

WATER   AIR   EARTH   FIRE

We studied the elements of nature—air, earth, fire, and water. These elements became the guiding iconography for the design of *Frozen 2* and a key inspiration for the film's narrative. The Water Spirit is inspired by old Norse myths. A wind spirit appears in some Scandinavian folk tales. There are myths about the giant boulders left over from the ice age that are scattered throughout Scandinavian forests and are said to have been thrown by rock trolls. The Fire Spirit was inspired by stories we heard about piles of timber that were lit on fire and salamanders ran out, making it seem like they were magical fire spirits. All of these elemental creatures come from the folktales, myths, and legends of the region.

—Chris Buck, director

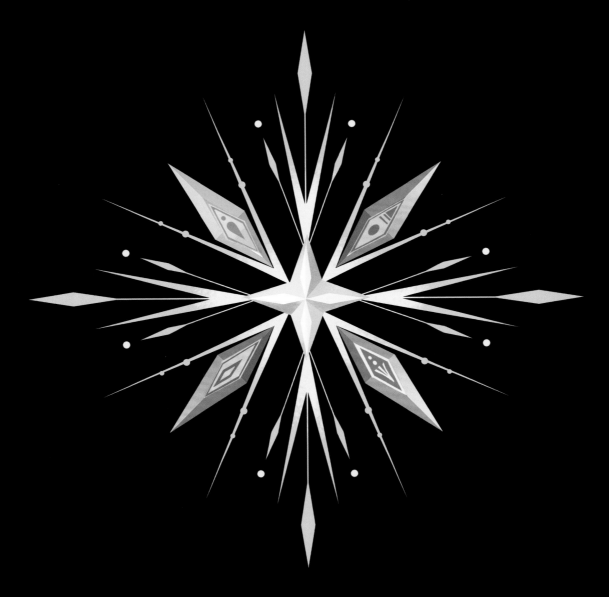

PART ONE

ARENDELLE

Several stories have taken place in the *Frozen* world now. To make sure the geography made sense logically in *Frozen 2*, we tweaked the design of Arendelle kingdom in subtle ways for accuracy. It feels more like an old European town now, with its own history. The streets and houses have a more logical layout. It feels like a real, permanent place.

—David Womersley, art director, environments

DAVID WOMERSLEY *Digital*

ARENDELLE NORTH

PAVING
VEGETABLES
BULBS
MOWN CEREAL
FRUIT ORCHARD
MOWN HAY

DAVID WOMERSLEY *Digital*

As we developed the village of Arendelle, we gave the streets names. Market Square is surrounded by the main streets of Klokkegate, which goes to the clock, and Hoydegate, which runs up a hill. Kongeligplas, or Royal Square, was so named because at one point there was going to be a royal statue there. Borgbro is the road that connects the main village to the castle. And Vindmolleveien is the windy road around the perimeter that has a windmill on it.

—David Womersley, art director, environments

DAVID WOMERSLEY *Digital*

DAVID WOMERSLEY *Digital*

The technology has improved since *Frozen*. We tried to make sure the essence of the original film—its look and feel—is retained, while also updating assets and elements where we can. For example, we're using a different renderer, called Disney's Hyperion Renderer, which increases the ability to make things feel like the material they actually are and to depict fine details we weren't able to show before. The film starts in Arendelle so audiences will see areas of the castle and village they've seen before, but there's more of a visual richness.

—Jack Fulmer, look development supervisor

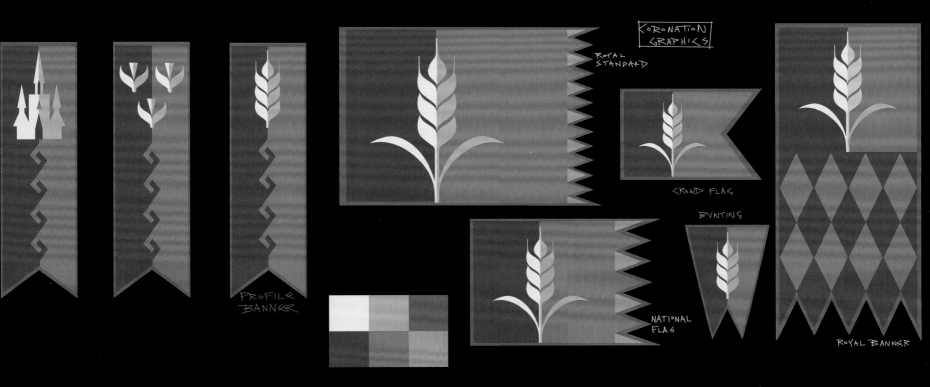

KORONATION GRAPHICS

ROYAL STANDARD

CROWD FLAG

BUNTING

PROFILE BANNER

NATIONAL FLAG

ROYAL BANNER

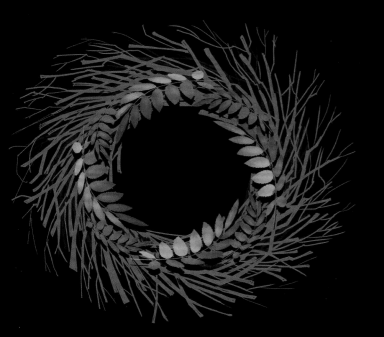

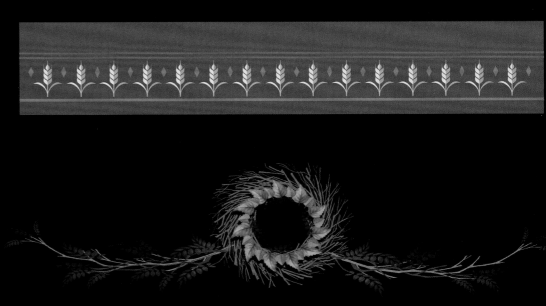

DAVID WOMERSLEY *Digital*

There was a version of the story where Arendelle Castle was washed away in a flood, and then rebuilt as a combination of the Northuldra and Arendellian styles. The castle's foundations became a series of islands linked with aerial bridges to various parts of the castle. Another version had the flow of water being reversed, which is why we designed the watermill.

—David Womersley, art director, environments

ANNA AND ELSA

JIN KIM *Pencil*

The challenge with a *Frozen* sequel was to find a good story that would allow these characters to navigate conflict in a way that's entertaining, interesting, and original. But it also had to feel like a continuation of the first film, not like we're inventing new emotional problems. Sequels should go deeper into the characters' emotional depths. *Frozen* was about reuniting the sisters and solving an immediate problem. *Frozen 2* takes place three years later, so we thought they would be at a point to deal with some unresolved issues from their childhoods.

—Marc Smith, story director

JIN KIM *Digital*

Overall, both Anna's and Elsa's outfits have more mature silhouettes. We lost the dropped V-shaped bodice in favor of a more natural waistline and included lots of fine detail that is more sober than decorative. Anna and Elsa are also very active in this film and need to be able to run and climb freely. Their travel dresses have an open panel to allow more movement. Underneath are leggings—think riding pants, not workout clothes or tights. Throughout, their clothing had to be consistent with the *Frozen* aesthetic and time period, faithful to the tone of the narrative, and true to the characters' styles, yet also be practical. And hopefully be really fabulous! It was incredibly challenging.

—Michael Giaimo, production designer

JIN KIM *Digital*

The characters are a little older; they're maturing. They have to deal with some pretty tough stuff. Animation can show some of that maturity in the characters' performances. It's subtle; the more internal a character is, the harder they are to animate. It's less about their movement, and more about showing their thinking.

—Becky Bresee, head of animation

ALL **JIN KIM** *Pencil, Digital*

Anna is trying to figure out where she fits in. Does she handle matters of state, or is she just there to throw parties and banquets? Does she get to have her own life, with her own wants and goals? And what about Kristoff? What's next for them as a couple?

—Marc Smith, story director

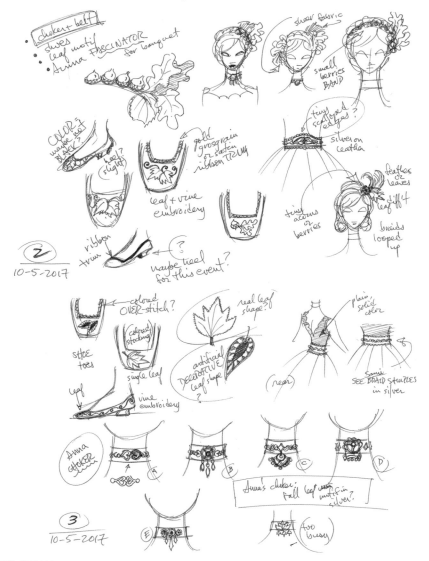

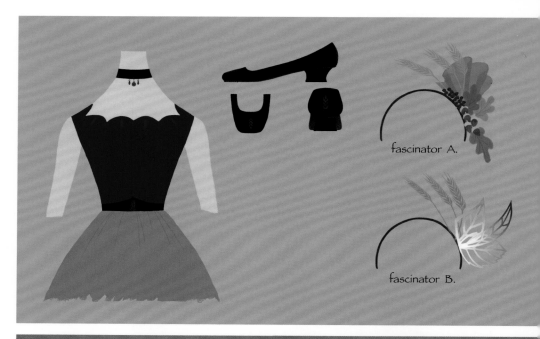

fascinator A.

fascinator B.

JEAN GILLMORE *Pencil*

TOP **JEAN GILLMORE** *Digital* | BOTTOM **GRISELDA SASTRAWINATA-LEMAY** *Digital*

Kristoff Intro Outfit

BRITTNEY LEE *Digital*

GRISELDA SASTRAWINATA-LEMAY *Digital*

Sketch annotations:
- GLOVES? and for balance (ombre gloves)
- back / FRONT
- ALL metal?
- BACK!
- (BACK) - no! make the front

TOP AND BOTTOM **JEAN GILLMORE** *Pencil, Digital*

ALL **GRISELDA SASTRAWINATA-LEMAY** *Digital*

Intro dress embroidery pattern.

main bodice pattern

cuff & scallop pattern

main skirt pattern

Short stem

long stem

main
floret row 1
floret row 2
floret row 3

take out row of florets as back scoops down

⊕ for skirt short stems:
> add florets as it gets longer toward the mid
> add pink dot in b/w the new florets & the original ones
> triangle at the end also get longer & bigger

add purple dot on the long stem

.. Intro Costume, undergarments

clean profile from structured corset

petticoat on top of corset

flatter on the front

more volume & fuller on the back.

We took the costuming to a new level of complexity in *Frozen 2*. We constructed the garments as if working with real cloth. For example, we created each individual panel that makes up the costumes, and essentially sewed them together and draped them on the characters. And the artists effectively hand-stitched each piece of rosemaling (traditional decorative flower motifs) and embroidery. They drew individual curves that represent each stitch on a pattern, say a crocus flower or a wheat pattern, and then stamped it on the costume. All of this helps the clothing feel more real.
—Alexander Alvarado, look development supervisor

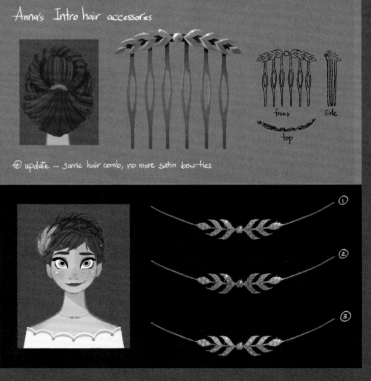

Anna's Intro hair accessories

front   side

top

⊕ update -- same hair comb, no more satin bow-ties

①
②
③

SASTRAWINATA-LEMAY *Digital*

Anna Final Travel Outfit

Anna's travel outfit was originally designed for Elsa, but as Elsa's character shifted, the outfit no longer reflected who she was. We loved the design, though, and used the original silhouette and colors intended for Elsa as the basis for Anna's main outfit. The skirt and cloak became shorter, and at one point we tried adding a bolero jacket. The clothes are functional for travel, but Anna still had to be recognizable as royalty, so they're very well made and have nice details.

—Jean Gillmore, visual development artist

Our initial designs for Anna in *Frozen 2* made her look too young. We tried to keep her double braids because they seemed iconic, but we ended up putting her hair in a single braid that wraps around at the nape of her neck then falls down freely, which helped give her a more mature look.

—Michael Giaimo, production designer

Anna -- double dutch braid -- 001

Anna hair -- half updo; twist

HAT?

rucksack behind

jacket has tiny FUR edge?

ANNA

Leather reinforced edge

KNAPSACK

large man's

(LEATHER) only loops

REAR

leather reinforced edge

FRONT

basket weave of birchbark (knapsack)

MAN'S

WOMAN'S

Basket weave of birch bark (knapsack)

Anna

KNAPSACK / RUCKSACK

case — low on back

Case - low on back

cloth or leather arm loops

smaller BIRCH BARK knapsack worn LOW on back, above waist

cloth or leather arm loops

smaller birch bark knapsack worn LOW on back, above waist

* DOUBLE-CHECK THIS ITEM

pg. 57 BUNAD book

Anna Travel Dress -- pattern

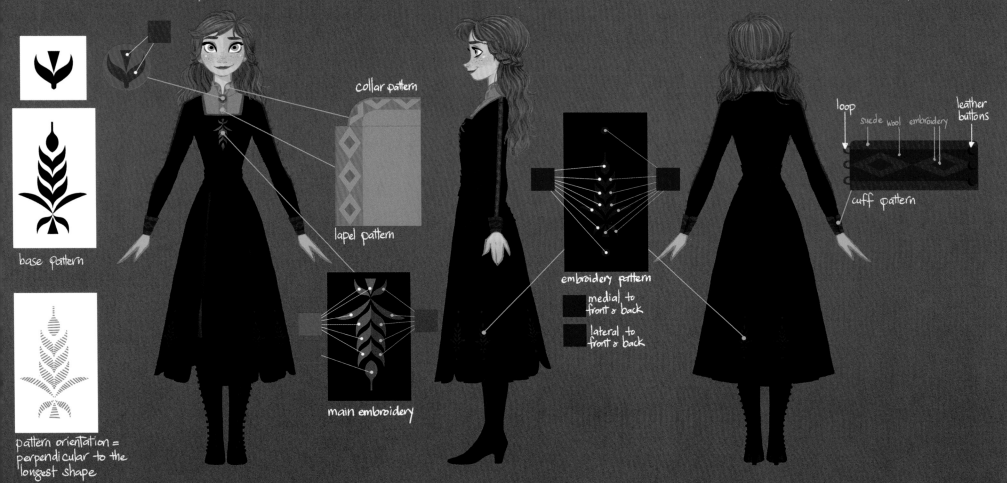

base pattern

pattern orientation = perpendicular to the longest shape

collar pattern

lapel pattern

main embroidery

embroidery pattern
medial to front & back

lateral to front & back

loop   suede   wool   embroidery   leather buttons

cuff pattern

Anna's maturity in this film can be tracked by her clothing. At the beginning of the film, she wears an ivory dress to represent her youthful, playful personality. But her travel outfit is mostly black to show that she is strong and knows when to be serious. Her final outfit combines who Anna is with what Arendelle is. It includes her signature black but also incorporates colors reminiscent of Elsa's coronation dress, as well as the greens and purples of Arendelle. Each outfit incorporates a curved, scalloped design somewhere, at the hem, sleeves, or across the bodice, and they become less rounded and more squared off as she matures.

—Griselda Sastrawinata-Lemay, visual development artist

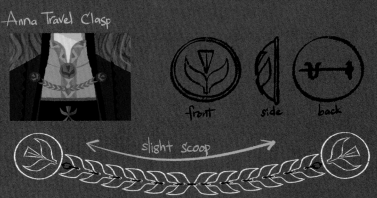

Anna Travel Clasp

front   side   back

slight scoop

ALL **GRISELDA SASTRAWINATA-LEMAY** *Pencil, Digital*

09.12.17

09.19.17

REAR   FRONT   "Banquet" ELSA

10.02.17   10.03.17   ELSA banquet gown w/ cloak

10.17.17

(w/ CLOAK)   Elsa   (dress behind)   rear

JEAN GILLMORE *Pencil, Digital*

Elsa Final Intro Outfit

Elsa is an artist, and almost everything she wears she has created using her magic. Her clothing reflects her own artistic sensibility, filtered through the time period, and is balanced between being made entirely of ice and the practical needs of each situation. In this film, Elsa's color palette has changed a little, to harmonize with the autumn palette. But if she wears anything too dark or warm or outside the spectrum of jewel tones, she stops looking like Elsa. The warmest she gets is a gray-lavender dress she wears at the beginning. It's the most real-world fabric she wears and is meant to fit into Arendelle more than anything she'd create for herself. We used lighter blues on a scale that moved into white to make her as light and ethereal as possible. Elsa also has more specularity than average people; she has a glow, a glitter to her. That's found in her clothing too, so there is always something that reflects light, such as sequins made of ice.

—Brittney Lee, visual development artist

ALL **BRITTNEY LEE** *Digital*

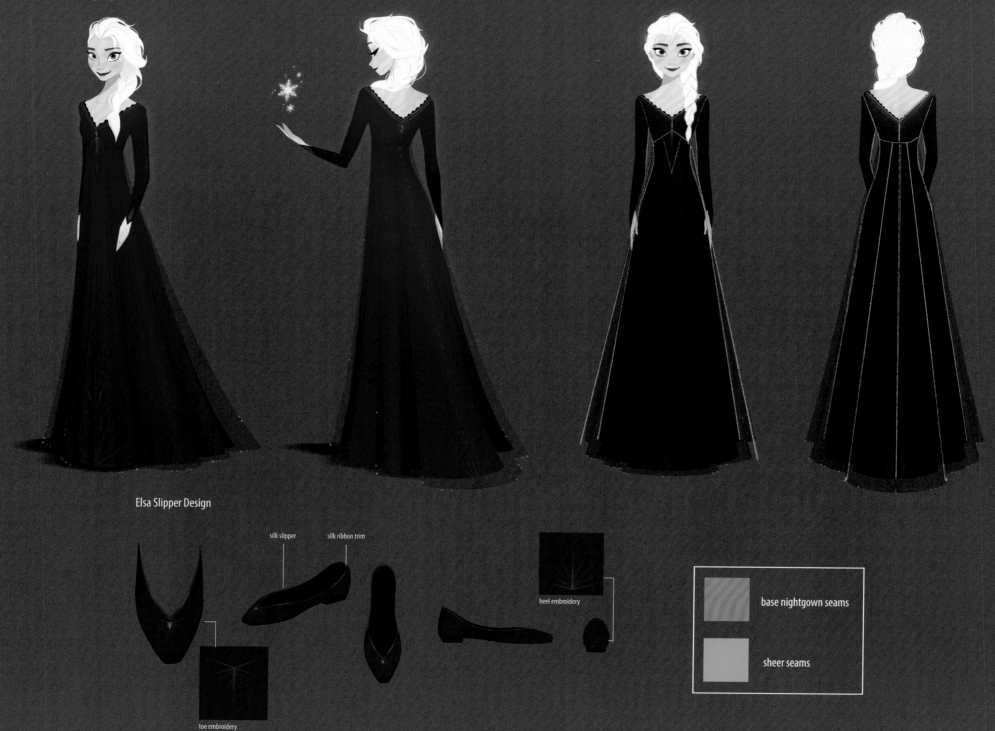

Elsa Slipper Design

silk slipper

silk ribbon trim

heel embroidery

toe embroidery

base nightgown seams

sheer seams

BRITTNEY LEE *Digital*

Elsa's travel outfit includes a coat, dress, pants, and boots. The coat has very structured shoulders and epaulets to telegraph that she is the queen—anyone who meets her knows she's the one in charge. The epaulets are meant to feel a bit like armor, imposing and strong, and were originally part of an earlier outfit that was designed but not used in the film. But they created such a beautiful silhouette that we wanted to incorporate them somewhere, and they ultimately became the element we designed her travel outfit around. Her dress is free-flowing and ethereal, made from a sheer silk tulle and covered in ice sequins from top to bottom. It's the garment that is most meant to look like magic, so there are no seams at the bust or neckline or hem.

—Brittney Lee, visual development artist

GRISELDA SASTRAWINATA-LEMAY *Digital*

Elsa's Original Travel Silhouette (Later Transferred to Anna)

We had to change Elsa's silhouette for travel. Every dress she's worn up to now has been floor-length, but in this film she treks through a forest, swims in the sea, and climbs a glacier. A longer hemline wouldn't be believable; it would drag on the ground and be cumbersome, so we had to raise the hemline of her dress. She's wearing boots, which are made of ice decorated with her snowflake design. Near the end of her journey, she goes barefoot.

—Michael Giaimo, production designer

JEAN GILLMORE *Pencil, Marker*

JEAN GILLMORE *Pencil*

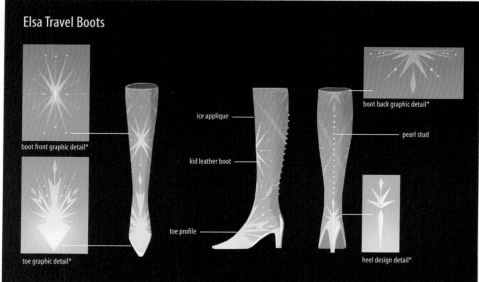

Elsa Travel Boots

boot front graphic detail*

toe graphic detail*

ice applique

kid leather boot

toe profile

boot back graphic detail*

pearl stud

heel design detail*

ABOVE AND RIGHT **BRITTNEY LEE** *Digital*

Elsa Final Travel Outfit

When we create things that don't exist in the real world, the design team often gives us references to the closest thing that does exist, and then we have to figure out how to use technology to build it. An example is Elsa's ice cape. The cape has to move in an authentic way based on the material it's made of, so we need to know what the texture and weight of the material is—in this case, ice crystals. Then we play with the cape in the computer until we get it to behave in a way that's believable. It's a lot of testing to find the right subtle balance. People are often surprised by how much time we spend on one particular outfit or hairstyle, but it's that attention to detail that we believe shows through in every frame of the movie. And it's exciting to realize something that we haven't seen before!

—Steve Goldberg, visual effects supervisor

JEAN GILLMORE *Pencil, Marker*

TOP **JEAN GILLMORE** *Pencil, Digital* | BOTTOM **GRISELDA SASTRAWINATA-LEMAY** *Digital*

Anna's epilogue outfit celebrates her new role as queen, while honoring the queens who came before her, Elsa and Iduna. Her tiara is a simple shape like Iduna's, but it incorporates more cut-out, negative space like Elsa's. Her dress includes Anna's signature black, which recalls Iduna's clothing, but it also has Arendelle green to echo Elsa's coronation dress. The dress's silhouette retains Anna's established shape language, but it is more streamlined. The exterior is a heavier, sturdier fabric to emphasize her new responsibility as queen, but the interior is light and flowy to preserve Anna's playfulness. And her cape incorporates her wheat motif along with the Arendelle crocus, signifying a new time in the kingdom's history.

—Griselda Sastrawinata-Lemay, visual development artist

GRISELDA SASTRAWINATA-LEMAY *Digital*

41

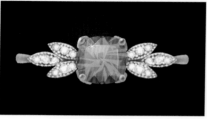

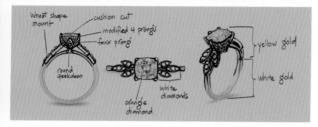

Anna's engagement ring is made from an orange diamond in a yellow- and white-gold setting inspired by the crocus and wheat motifs that appear throughout *Frozen 2*. I imagined that Kristoff was drawn to the stone, which the trolls dug up for him, because orange diamonds are rare and the vibrant color resembles Anna's rich, auburn hair.

—Griselda Sastrawinata-Lemay, visual development artist

Anna's epilogue outfit is made up of multiple fabrics, including wool, velvet, and silk, and is heavily embroidered. Green, purple, and black are the main colors, and the Arendelle wheat symbol is the primary motif. Velvet, silk, and embroidery all have anisotropic highlights—a shine that has direction and movement to it—which provides contrast to the matte wool. The needlework of the embroidery has to stand out against the other materials, but no one material or color should draw the eye more than the rest. We try to maintain a truth to materials, and each has unique qualities that ultimately have to work together.

—Ian Butterfield, look development artist

Elsa's epilogue costume signifies her final transformation. The main body of her dress is white velvet as a nod to her snow and ice origins, and the extended yards of organza in her cape and dress hem suggest the magical, elusive character she has always been. But the curved bodice silhouette indicates her newfound confidence, and the decorative adornments throughout the outfit, which display the iconography of the four elements, symbolically denote her deep connection to nature itself.

—Michael Giaimo, production designer

TOP LEFT **JEAN GILLMORE** *Pencil* | ABOVE **MICHAEL GIAIMO** *Digital*

Elemental Gem Hues

water

wind

earth

fire

We designed the unity snowflake symbol as a visual manifestation of Elsa's connection to nature—she is the center from which each of the four elements of nature emanates.
—Michael Giaimo, production designer

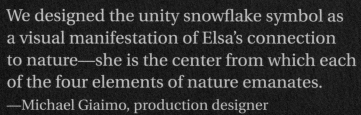

ALL **BRITTNEY LEE** *Digital*

Elsa Epilogue Bodice Material/Detail Reference

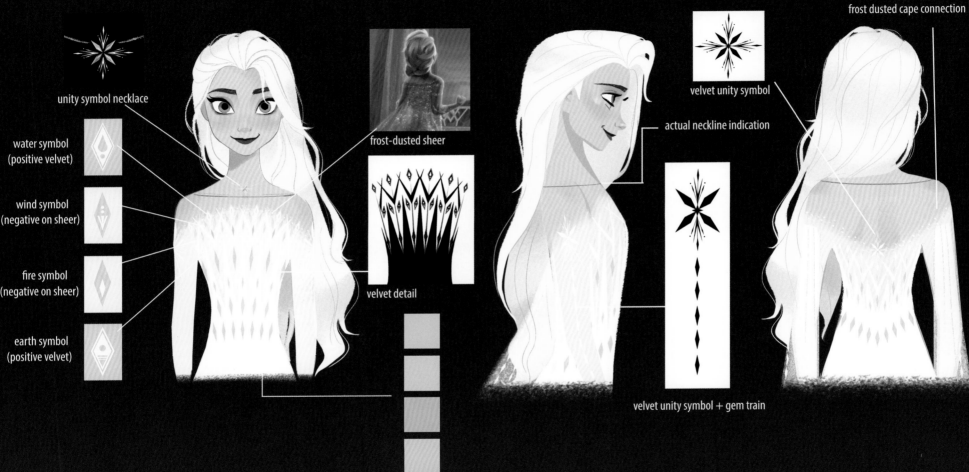

frost dusted cape connection

unity symbol necklace

water symbol
(positive velvet)

wind symbol
(negative on sheer)

fire symbol
(negative on sheer)

earth symbol
(positive velvet)

frost-dusted sheer

velvet detail

bodice gem hues

velvet unity symbol

actual neckline indication

velvet unity symbol + gem train

BRITTNEY LEE *Digital*

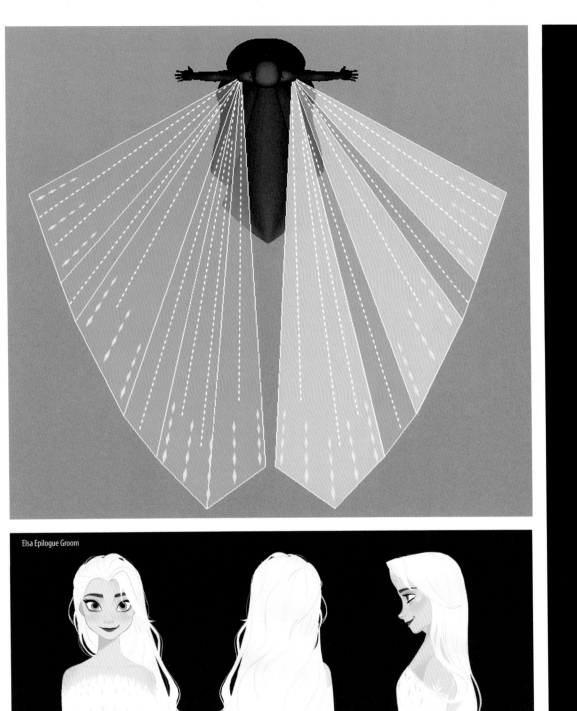

Elsa Epilogue Groom

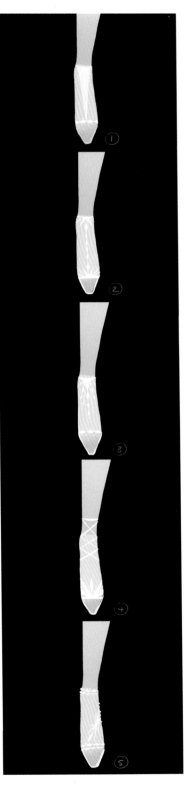

ALL **BRITTNEY LEE** *Digital*

We retained Elsa's shape language but changed the design language to better reflect her journey in this film. So rather than using snowflakes as Elsa's signature motif, we used the elements, which are visually depicted as a diamond shape. The color of each diamond denotes which element it represents—air, earth, fire, water—in jewel tones from warm to cool. As Elsa discovers her connection to the elements, they become part of her aesthetic and appear in her clothing. By the end she incorporates the full spectrum of elements as well as her snowflake into her outfit.

—Brittney Lee, visual development artist

BRITTNEY LEE *Digital*

Kristoff and Sven

Kristoff's clothing has colors and patterning that reflect the autumn palette of this film and connect him more to Arendelle. The wheat motif and antler symbol often appear in his clothes. He has more costume changes in this film than he's ever had before, and his final outfit was designed to complement Anna's final outfit so that they look good together. He cleans up well!

—Griselda Sastrawinata-Lemay, visual development artist

It's autumn, and Sven still has a fuzzy coating on his antlers. His harness has an autumnal wheat motif, which connects him to Anna and Arendelle. That motif is incorporated into a lot of the costumes and the banners and decorative elements in Arendelle.

—Bill Schwab, art director, characters

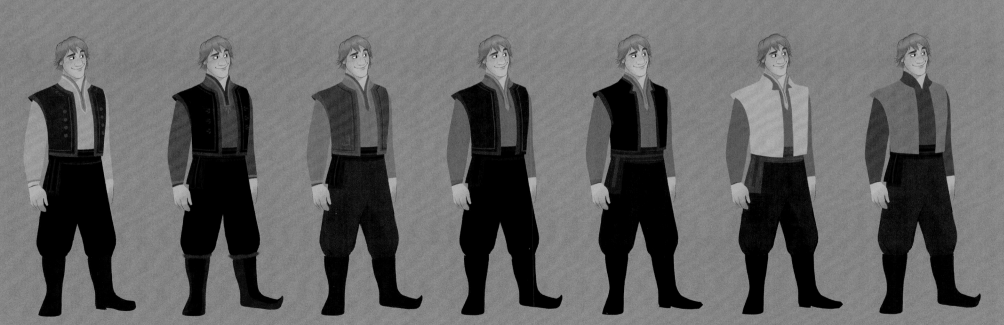

OLAF

In the Enchanted Forest, Olaf wanders off on his own and encounters the elemental spirits. We see the results of what the spirits are doing—Earth Giants throwing boulders, fire jumping from tree to tree—but we don't actually see the spirits yet. They're observing, not attacking Olaf, but there are moments where it could seem a little threatening, and it's definitely bizarre. Olaf is confused— he doesn't know if he should be scared or not—but he shrugs it off and tells himself it will all make sense when he's older.

—Dan Abraham, story artist

"WHEN I AM OLDER"

ARENDELLIANS

Since Elsa became queen and opened the gates to the castle, people from all over the world have come to visit Arendelle. Many have moved there, creating an even more diverse Arendelle filled with international characters.

—Peter Del Vecho, producer

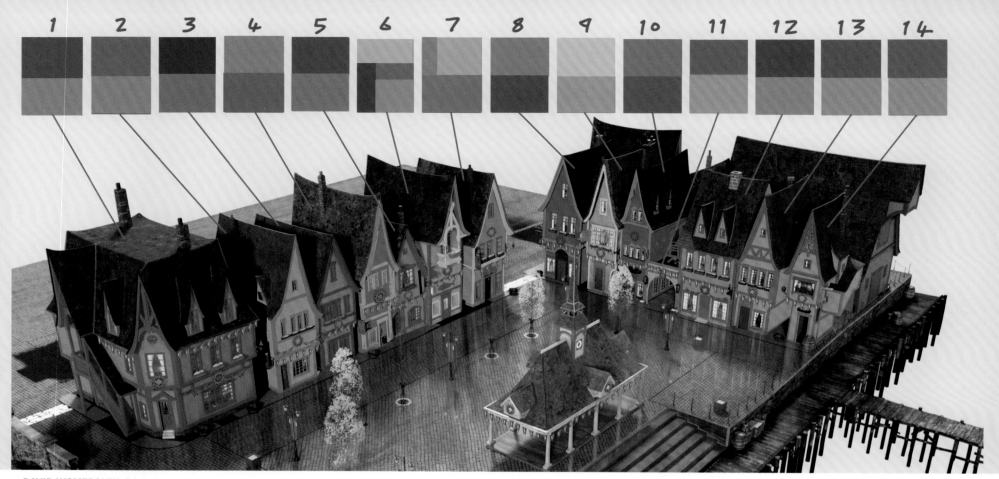

DAVID WOMERSLEY *Digital*

Because *Frozen 2* takes place in the fall, we updated the characters and environments of Arendelle to reflect the season. Castle staff and soldiers, buildings and banners, and all of the attendant accessories had to be carefully orchestrated to achieve the appropriate look for the kingdom.

—Brittney Lee, visual development artist

ALL **GRISELDA SASTRAWINATA-LEMAY** *Digital*

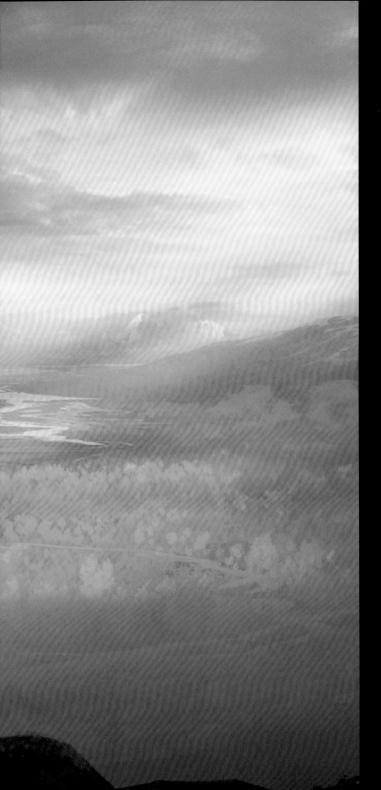

PART TWO

AIR

For the elemental characters like the Wind Spirit, the Water Spirit, the Fire Spirit, and the Earth Giants, there's a blurred line: Is it a character, or is it part of the environment? We had to draw inspiration for eac[h] from its environment in order to convey that it's mad[e] out of whatever element it is—air, water, fire, earth— but we also had to create characters that could give emotional performances. Animation, effects, look de[sign,] design, modeling, rigging—all these departments col[-] laborated very closely on all these characters.

—Sean Jenkins, head of environments

LISA KEENE, *Digital*

NCHANTED OREST

Enchanted Forest looks different in various
ions as the characters travel through it on
journey. It had to have emotional context
almost be a character in its own right.

vid Womersley, art director, environments

LISA KEENE *Digital*

JAMES FINCH *Digital*

It's difficult in CG to make an organic environment look appealing. A forest can look like a salad bowl—nice elements but without any design structure. Trees can be designed from one side to look beautiful in two dimensions, but how do you maintain that shape language as the camera rotates around them as 3-D objects? We used careful placement of branches and leaf canopies on individual trees that were then combined into groups to bring a rhythm and organization to the organic nature of the forest and keep it from looking haphazard. It's not architectural, but it has structure; it's not so designed that the audience notices it, but they feel it.

—Michael Giaimo, production designer

LISA KEENE & JUSTIN CRAM *Digital*

The Enchanted Forest is surrounded by a dome of misty fog. It creates an almost magical portal the characters must cross to enter the forest. As they pass through it, a sparkle effect occurs, like static electricity. It's real fog, made of water particles, but it's subtly colorful, with each element's signature hue reflected in it, from purple to cyan.

The effects challenge was to build fog that is ethereal but solid. It had to look natural but behave somewhat unnaturally to cue viewers that it's not regular mist and it's not just water vapor. It's not a falling mist; it's crawling upward, pulled from the environment around it, and it is a massive, thick dome that covers where much of the story takes place. Another challenge was preserving the crisp detail in the mist, the fine edges of a solid object but on something that is moving like a fluid. Because it's not a mist that dissipates into a haze, it has a clear definition that shows it is an impenetrable barrier.

—Jesse Erickson, effects animation lead

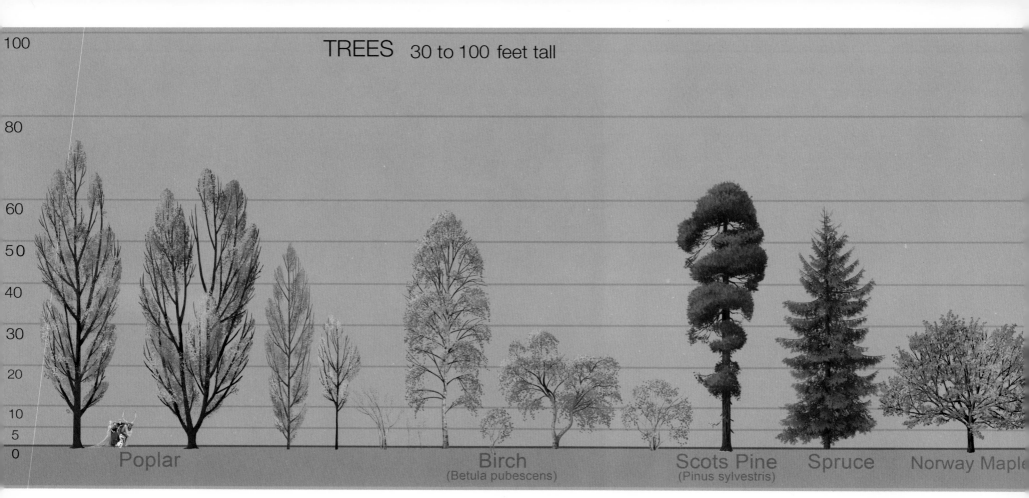

TREES 30 to 100 feet tall

100

80

60
50

40

30

20

10
5
0

Poplar

Birch
(Betula pubescens)

Scots Pine
(Pinus sylvestris)

Spruce

Norway Maple

JIM FINN *Digital*

The production design team started by referencing
tree species that would grow in this region of the world,
and then reshaped them into Eyvind Earle–inspired
silhouettes that interact with one another. Taken
together, the trees create a forest that is more composed;
the trees are layered and placed in specific ways so,
though inspired by nature, the forest is really stylized.
—Sean Jenkins, head of environments

Silver Birch

Aspen
(Populus tremula)

Rowan

Alder
Gray Alder (Alnus incana)

Juniper
(Juniperus communis)

We consulted a botanist from Norway about what grows where and then chose a limited suite of trees and vegetation to depict. Those were the puzzle pieces. We designed small vignettes with those species, stacking them and making tree islands in groupings that are attractive and work aesthetically from different angles. Then those could be multiplied, and rotated so each would look different, and then layered to create a huge forest.

—Lisa Keene, co-production designer

Forests are not just trees. There are so many variations of what's on the ground, particularly in the autumn: earth, roots, rocks, pebbles, fallen foliage, various species of vegetation. We had to select what to include and then organize those elements in a way that is believable yet naturalistic. We were inspired by what we saw on our research trip, particularly hiking in Finland and Norway. We observed the ground cover and re-created many of those species, including crowberries, bilberries, cloudberries, fireweed—things you only observe if you go to a particular place.

—Michael Giaimo, production designer

MARC SMITH & JENNIFER LEE *Frozen 2 Research Trip Photos*

ABOVE AND RIGHT **MAC GEORGE** *Digital*

MONKSHOOD

TOP AND BOTTOM **MAC GEORGE** *Digital*

Mattias

Mattias is a warm, heroic character. He's very pragmatic but he's also an optimist, so he and Anna connect quickly. He is the one who tells Anna that when things get difficult, you just have to pick yourself up and do what's right. These words of wisdom inspire Anna in her darkest moment.

—Peter Del Vecho, producer

ABOVE **BILL SCHWAB** *Digital* | RIGHT **GRISELDA SASTRAWINATA-LEMAY** *Digital*

Mattias wears a military uniform that is based on the clothing worn by the Arendelle guards. The colors, material, and pattern motifs connect him to Arendelle, but to emphasize his importance and to help him stand out, his jacket is shorter and he has epaulets and a cape. He's been in the Enchanted Forest for many years but continues to take his leadership responsibilities seriously and meticulously maintains his uniform.

—Griselda Sastrawinata-Lemay, visual development artist

ABOVE AND RIGHT **BILL SCHWAB** *Digital*

ALL **BILL SCHWAB** *Digital*

SHIPWRECK

We implied in the first film that Anna's and Elsa's parents' ship sank in the Southern Seas, so when they find it in the Enchanted Forest, it's a shock. It's a royal ship based on those made in the 1830s and '40s, but in *Frozen* we only saw the ship in a couple of shots. Now we go inside the ship, so we designed the decks and interior details. The stained-glass windows with beautiful light filtering through them provide a very operatic feeling to the scene, which is further enhanced by having trees all around the ship that are more depressed-looking, a little more twisted and forlorn.

—David Womersley, art director, environments

BOTH PAGES **JIM MARTIN** *Digital*

AGNARR AND IDUNA

Queen Iduna is Anna's and Elsa's mother. King Agnarr is their father, and Runeard is their paternal grandfather. We tried to find physical features to show that they're all related, such as Anna's freckles and auburn hair, and Elsa's eye color and a bit of her bone structure.

—Bill Schwab, art director, characters

RUNEARD

AGNARR

IDUNA

ANNA

ELSA

TOP **BILL SCHWAB** *Digital*
MIDDLE AND BOTTOM **BRITTNEY LEE** *Digital*

BRITTNEY LEE *Digital*

Anna's and Elsa's mother, Queen Iduna, had to endure many emotional wounds, but she's a nurturing mother who put her family first. She didn't speak much in the first film; but, all along, she was looking for ways to help her daughters, as well as the people she came from, to help heal their broken lands. Anna and Elsa probably wouldn't succeed in this journey if not for all their mother did for them.

—Jennifer Lee, director and screenwriter

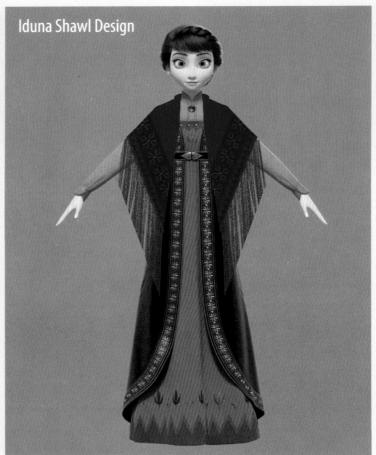

Iduna Shawl Design

BRITTNEY LEE *Digital*

Iduna's shawl provides visual clues to her past and to Anna's and Elsa's futures. The garment is Northuldra, passed down through the maternal side of the family. The iconography on it represents all four elements that will eventually lead Elsa to discover her destiny.

—Michael Giaimo, production designer

Agnarr has a very prominent nose, not so much that it's *big* but it's long in proportion to his face. He has a younger, longer version of the hairstyle he wore in the first film.

—Bill Schwab, art director, characters

Young Agnarr

GRISELDA SASTRAWINATA-LEMAY *Digital*

Everyone ages differently, but certain things seem universal: Midsections tend to spread, posture changes, noses and ears grow for our whole lives. But the essence of the character is the same; and it isn't one thing in particular—though things like eye shape and bone structure really help. We looked at the designs for Queen Iduna and King Agnarr from the first film and talked about what we wanted to preserve in order to make them look twenty-five years younger in this film.

—Bill Schwab, art director, characters

JEAN GILLMORE *Digital*　　　　　　**HYUN MIN LEE** *Digital*

BILL SCHWAB *Digital*

Aspects could mimic
Elsa's Travel outfit

wool undergarments
(never see in totality)

ASPECTS
could
mimic
Elsa's travel
outfit

IDUNA

wool
undergarments
(never see in
totality)

belt?

"boat" neck

patchwork band
leggings

patchwork band
leggings

①
8-25-2017

JEAN GILLMORE *Pencil*

As a child, Iduna was one with nature, comfortable with
the Wind Spirit, happy and free. She's fun-loving and out-
going like Anna, she enjoys the magic of the world like
Elsa, and there's a thoughtfulness to her that both Anna
and Elsa have. Young Iduna is what Anna and Elsa might
have been like if they had grown up together having fun.
It's her pure, core being, without all the propriety.
—Hyun Min Lee, visual development artist

BILL SCHWAB *Digital*

The simulation team focused on getting the costumes to fit better and look and move more like real cloth. This allowed the design of the material to be supported by the intended motion of the material, and both of those things to work with the overall animation goals.

—Gregory Smith, head of characters

BILL SCHWAB *Digital*

BLACK AND WHITE **HYUN MIN LEE** *Digital*

Wind Spirit

When we first started designing the Wind Spirit, we thought it might sometimes form an identifiable face, but we moved away from that. It's not anthropomorphic; it's nature, it's wind. We only "see" it by how it causes other things to react, like hair or fabric rippling, or through forest matter it blows around.

—Michael Giaimo, production designer

LISA KEENE *Digital*

84

ALL **ANNETTE MARNAT** *Digital*

The Wind Spirit provided a unique challenge in my career. The filmmakers wanted it to be more natural, not anthropomorphized, so it couldn't have a face, yet it still had to communicate emotion. The wind itself can't be seen, but you can see the effect wind has on objects and the environment. We did several tests with that in mind, using leaves and sticks and other things to create shapes and movement that expressed emotion. We had playful moments with Olaf or Sven, and a quieter moment with Elsa as it swirled around her, blowing her hair and clothing in communication with her.

—Mark Henn, animator

BILL SCHWAB *Digital*

TOP AND BOTTOM **JAMES WOODS** *Digital*

In trying to realize the wind in CG, we were inspired by dust devils, which are delightful because they form and disappear and then reappear somewhere else. We started out pretty heavy-handed, but as we tested different ideas, we saw that less is more—we experimented with how little particulate we could show in the air, whether it's leaves or fireweed fluff or pollen, and still convey the wind. We did a preproduction test and uncovered all kinds of things we couldn't predict, and we learned a lot before creating any footage for the film.

—Steve Goldberg, visual effects supervisor

ALL **BILL SCHWAB** *Digital*

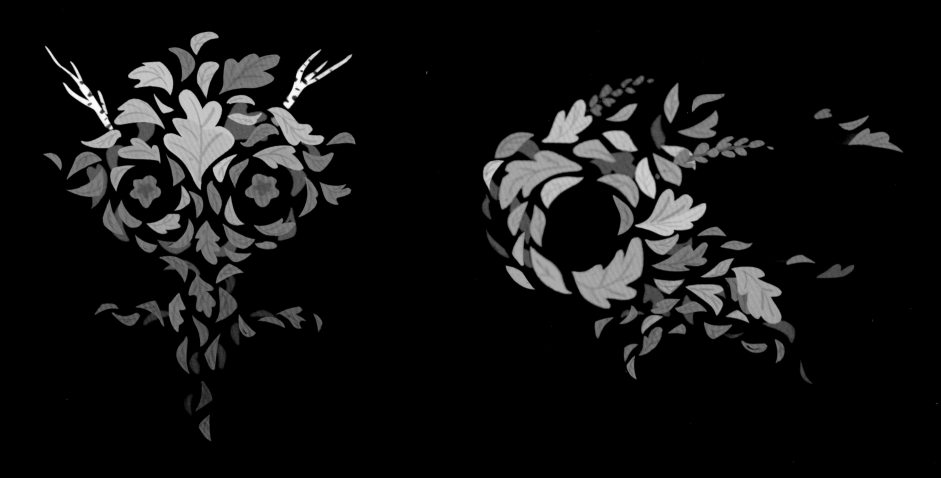

BILL SCHWAB *Digital*

The Wind Spirit is a character you can't actually see,
so it has to do all of its emoting and communicating
through how it interacts with its environment. We use
twigs, leaves, berries, seedpods. We used dandelions
at first but then learned they don't really grow in
Scandinavia so we used the fireweed plant, which has
a great color palette and is tipped with fluffy poofs.
—Sean Jenkins, head of environments

GRISELDA SASTRAWINATA-LEMAY *Digital*

In many films, the workflow between animation and tech anim often goes like this: An animator animates a character, say, flinging her cape; the heads of animation do draw-overs to show the adjustments we'd make to achieve the actual look we want; then that goes to tech anim, who do their take on it; and the two departments might go back and forth a little bit. But with the Wind Spirit, who is a character you can't see, we needed tech anim to show us where the wind was blowing in the environment so we could animate that effect on the other characters. We had to help each other so the pieces would fit together and time out perfectly. It was an extraordinarily collaborative team effort.
—Tony Smeed, head of animation

~ PART THREE ~
# EARTH

The elements are characters that are half living creature, half environment; and their designs and performances were created across several departments. The teams got together to brainstorm—and it was a domino effect. An idea would be suggested, and everyone's imaginations would flare, sparking a crazy idea that wouldn't have come up otherwise. The evolution of each elemental character was subtle day by day, but if you played the months back at high speed, you'd see the characters evolve from abstract ideas to unique and sophisticated characters.

—Becky Bresee, head of animation

JAMES FINCH *Digital*

YELANA

Yelana, the Northuldra leader, feels a deep responsibility for her people and has a sense of larger purpose. She has long, light-silver hair that sets her apart visually. It's worn in a style that resembles a crown, which gives her a regal bearing that is our nod to her status as an elder.

—Nick Orsi, visual development artist

BILL SCHWAB *Digital*

BRITTNEY LEE *Digital*

Yelana's and Honeymaren's clothing uses primarily hexagonal honeycomb shapes in accessories and patterning. The outfit consists of a base layer of wool pants and shirt, for warmth. A separate piece of wool is wrapped around the bottom of each pants leg to affix the pant to the boot and provide extra warmth. Over all of it is a coat and hat, and a belt with grommets that are used to carry tools and other necessities.

—Griselda Sastrawinata-Lemay, visual development artist

TOP **BILL SCHWAB** *Digital* | BOTTOM **NICK ORSI** *Digital*

Honeymaren and Ryder

Honeymaren and Ryder are sister and brother, so they need to feel related yet different. Ryder is a high-energy, playful guy with a broad smile and easy laugh. He has a deep connection to reindeer, just like Kristoff, so they're fast friends. Honeymaren is more stoic, a strong leader. Both are very athletic and comfortable in their environment.

—Bill Schwab, art director, characters

Our filmmaking team's research trip stops in Norway and Finland connected us with so many wonderful people from all over the region, including the indigenous Sámi people with whom we collaborated to design the final costumes for Honeymaren, Ryder, and Yelana. We are grateful for their partnership.

—Peter Del Vecho, producer

ALL **BRITTNEY LEE** *Digital*

The Northuldra are very much connected with nature. They spend much of their time living and working outdoors and have adapted to thrive in all conditions. We wanted their look to reflect that.

—Chad Stubblefield, character model supervisor

BOTTOM RIGHT **BILL SCHWAB** *Digital*
ALL OTHER BLACK AND WHITE **JIN KIM** *Digital*

TOP AND BOTTOM **BILL SCHWAB** *Digital*

95

NORTHULDRA

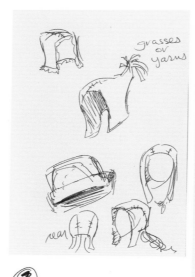

9-18-2017

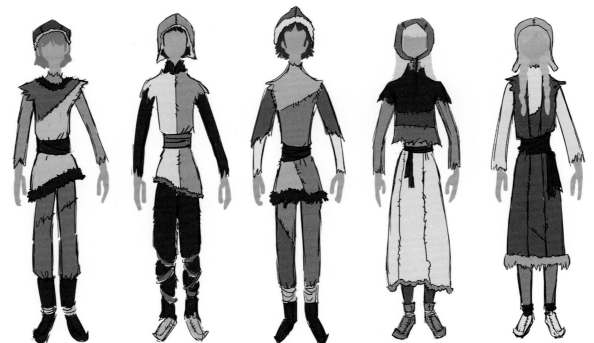

JEAN GILLMORE *Pencil, Digital*　　　　　　　　Early Costume Exploration—Northuldra

The Northuldra are a peaceful people. There is an athleticism and swiftness to their movement that sets them apart from our other characters.

—Becky Bresee, head of animation

TOP AND BOTTOM **BILL SCHWAB** *Digital*

TOP AND BOTTOM **JIN KIM** *Digital*

We started pretty broad in designing the other reindeer in the film, with more caricatured proportions. But, ultimately, they really just had to feel like a herd. Sven stands out because he's bigger, but the Northuldra reindeer do feel like they're related to him.

—Bill Schwab, art director, characters

JAMES WOODS *Digital*

JUSTIN CRAM *Digital*

EARTH GIANTS

For the Earth Giants, we wanted to do something
inventive. The environments team and character
designers developed the Earth Giants together,
because they are part character and part environment.
We wanted them to feel like they came directly out
of the rock face, as if they're part of it, not just living
on it. Usually when something is anthropomorphized,
it means giving it human anatomy—head, facial
features, symmetrical arms and legs—but we wanted
to challenge that assumption, so even if they have
two arms or legs, one is short and the other is long.
Roots are the connective tissue of their joints.

—Michael Giaimo, production designer

JAMES FINCH *Digital*

JAMES FINCH *Digital*

The Earth Giants are like mountains; they're huge and made of earth and rock. They blend into the environment they're sleeping in, and each has slightly different rock types and patterning. They've been asleep for decades, so one side is verdant and green, while the other side is covered in roots and whatever's been under the rock during that time. When they rise from their reclining sleeping position, we see that trees are growing off the sides of their bodies.

—Luis Labrador, environment model supervisor

BILL SCHWAB *Digital*

BILL SCHWAB *Digital*

The Earth Giants are made of rock and they're asymmetrical, both of which drastically affect the way they move. And they're heavy, so the animation has to convey their size and weight.

—Tony Smeed, head of animation

We didn't want to do the expected slow motion often seen with big creatures. So to help depict the Earth Giants' scale, we show little pieces of rock and debris falling from them. Trees that grow on them move independently of the giants' movement. They disturb the earth as they move, leaving enormous footprints.

—Marlon West, head of effects, animation

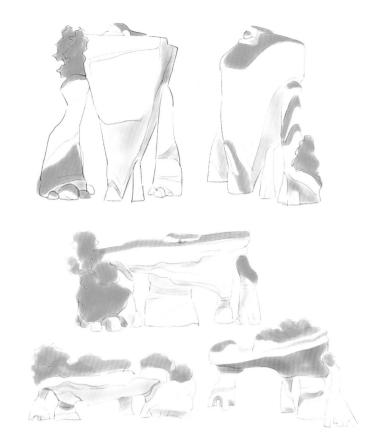

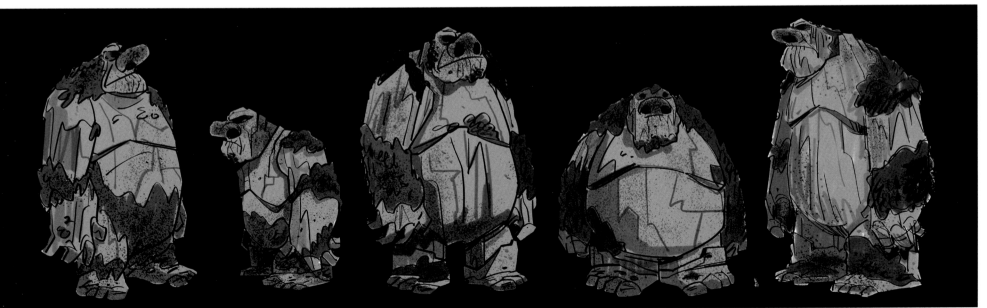

TOP LEFT AND RIGHT **NICK ORSI** *Digital* | BOTTOM **BILL SCHWAB** *Digital*

~ PART FOUR ~

FIRE

The fire in *Frozen 2* is magical, so it didn't have to look like real fire. That gave us license to really stylize it and give it a sense of whimsy. But like all the effects we created, it still had to fit into the *Frozen* world and support the production design, which has an elegance. And for every shot and sequence, we ask ourselves: What is the emotional tone of this sequence, and how can effects support that? It's not just about what would naturally happen in the real world.

—Dale Mayeda, head of effects, animation

LISA KEENE *Digital*

FIRE SPIRIT

In some European folklore, the salamander is connected to fire. In *Frozen 2*, our Fire Spirit is a little salamander that looks adorable and cute and safe—something Olaf might want to be friends with. But it quickly transforms into something terrifying, and mayhem ensues. The fire it creates is not the kind of fire we associate with the real world—it's enchanted fire, with unusual colors.

—Bill Schwab, art director, characters

BILL SCHWAB *Digital*

JAMES WOODS *Digital*

Every element is represented as a diamond shape, and the fire element evokes a candle flame—it's a little fire within the diamond. Salamanders often have naturally occurring patterns on their skin, so we channeled the fire element design into the Fire Spirit's pattern. This design appears on the Salamander's back, almost like a stamp, with related color and patterning around it. The fire element pattern can be seen in some of the flame licks that the Fire Spirit emits.

—Nick Orsi, visual development artist

All of the characters and environments that we built had to support the film's aesthetic vision, but they were also primarily story driven. When we first heard that the Fire Spirit would be a character, all we knew about it was it would involve "fantasy fire" and "magical flames." We didn't know what that would look like until the directors figured out the Fire Spirit's story function. And that can be really fun—because when things aren't explicitly spelled out yet, it gives us artists a moment to just imagine what it could be. And then when we start seeing storyboards, ideas really start flying.

—Jack Fulmer, look development supervisor

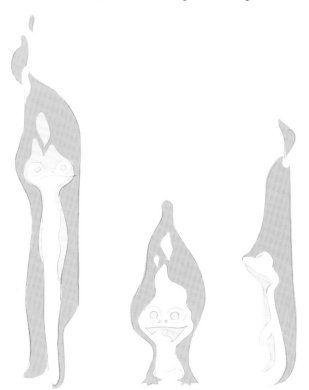

NICK ORSI *Digital*

LISSA TREIMAN *Digital*

In each encounter Elsa has with an element, she learns more about how to interact with the spirits, how to become the bridge that will connect them all. The Fire Spirit is the second spirit she meets, and it appears in a moment of conflict between the Northuldra and the Arendellians in the forest. It is petulant, angry, scared, frantic; it emits pink fire. It's magical fire, so we didn't want it to be the typical orange color, and since Elsa's ice powers are blue, pink felt like a good contrast to that.
—Lissa Treiman, story artist

LOST CAVERNS

The Lost Caverns are a sheer drop at the end of a waterfall, with no way out. They are a dark pit full of black rocks, which is difficult to design. You have to use light and atmosphere to give it visual depth. It's where Anna is when she's at her lowest emotional point in the film, and it feels like crying. It's very tearful with dripping water.

—Lisa Keene, co-production designer

LEFT **LISA KEENE** *Digital* | ABOVE **DAVID WOMERSLEY** *Digital*

"THE NEXT RIGHT THING"

The emotion of a scene dictates the cinematography. How the camera moves and how a scene is lit help tell the story and support what the characters are feeling. The sequence for the song "The Next Right Thing" is a good example. It starts off with Anna at her lowest emotional moment. In the beginning, the camera is very still and wide, which makes Anna look small and vulnerable, and the lighting is very gray, dark, and contrast-y. Those two things convey her state of mind and evoke the same emotion in the audience. As Anna slowly starts moving, the camera becomes a little more active, and lighting introduces a literal ray of hope—a little glimmer from the opening she's heading toward. Once she gets out of the Lost Caverns, the camera motion increases and the cutting gets quicker, ending with a big 360º camera rotation and bright, sunny lighting. The sequence goes from a really dark, static environment with a pulled-back camera to active close-ups on a beautiful day, which parallels Anna's emotional arc.
—Scott Beattie, director of cinematography, layout

~ PART FIVE ~
WATER

Elsa's magic comes from and is a part of nature. Her powers are connected to water. As we looked into the science of water, we learned about the concept that water has memory. Water dissolves other substances and absorbs part of everything that passes through it, so in a sense it really holds our history. All the water we have is all the water we ever had or will have. It was incredibly powerful to stand on a giant glacier and realize it held history—and even more incredible to think Elsa was connected to that.

—Peter Del Vecho, producer

LISA KEENE *Digital*

LISA KEENE *Digital*

DARK SEA

Elsa stands on the Black Beach as she looks out at
the Dark Sea, knowing she has to cross it to get to
Ahtohallan. The beach is inspired by Reynisfjara
Black Sand Beach in Iceland. It was a challenging
space to design because the scene takes place at
midnight, the sand is black, and the sea is dark.
It's lit only by lightning and other ethereal things.

—David Womersley, art director, environments

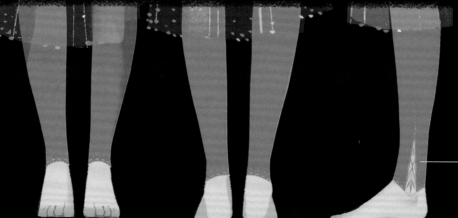

BRITTNEY LEE *Digital*

*cutout on outer ankle only

ankle embroidery detail

As Elsa crosses the Dark Sea, she encounters many different weather conditions—dry, wet, windy, underwater—and each situation has its own visual look, style, and quality of motion. She's wearing pants, and there is enough material in her dress to allow it to clear away from her body, out of the way of her legs and feet as she's running. This gave us freedom to open up the drama of the dress, let all the elaborate folds un-accordion out behind her like a ballerina's dress, moving in a light, floaty, ethereal way. Her hair goes from dry through various stages of wetness, from braided to a ponytail that by the end has pieces pulled out around her face. She's not her normal contained self.

—Dave Suroviec, technical animation supervisor

WATER SPIRIT

The Water Spirit was one of the most challenging characters to design. It's a fantasy creature, so we didn't have to be overly literal about anatomy, but it still had to look like a horse. We had to figure out the right balance between horse anatomy and the properties of water. How does that manifest in the actual body of the horse, compared to mane and tail? How much stylization should it have? What does it look like both above and below water? Since it's made of water, internal parts of the horse are transparent, yet it also has to look powerful, and those two things are often at odds. On top of that, the character is foreboding, mysterious, dangerous; and yet at the end it acquiesces to Elsa; it respects her. It's like nature itself—sometimes kind and forgiving, sometimes catastrophic and devastating. This character had to represent all of that, and do so without a lot of screen time.

—Michael Giaimo, production designer

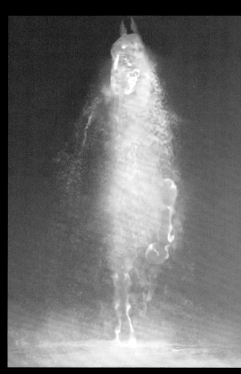

ALL **LISA KEENE** *Digital*

The Water Spirit has properties that allow it to be seen underwater. Even in water, it's got to look like it's made of water, somewhat amorphous, legs forming and disappearing. Every time it moves underwater, there's a glow that trails behind it so it always appears in silhouette. Initially, it had a blue color, but we softened it to a very subtle gray that appears slightly violet, along with gray-blues and gray-greens. Its extremities are transparent, and there's a dance of light along its edges. When you allow light to hit the leading edge of an object, it sparkles. Our eyes wouldn't see that in a still image, but when it's moving our minds fill in the gaps, and we see the shape of the creature. In motion, we were able to depict something we couldn't illustrate.

—Lisa Keene, co-production designer

ALL **JAMES WOODS** *Digital*

Our initial test of the Water Spirit had a lot of water coming from the mane and tail because it seemed like those would be areas with more action, where we could show that it's a creature made of water. But in the end the gushing water became more of a gentle fountain with really subtle tells, like minimal surface motion and far fewer droplets than we initially tried.

—Steve Goldberg, visual effects supervisor

BILL SCHWAB *Digital*

The Water Spirit looks different on land than it does in water. On land, the effects occur more around the edges of the horse; particles of water called spindrift move and blow off of it, similar to what happens to crashing ocean waves. Underwater, the effects happen inside the horse; there's no spindrift, and it has an internal iridescence, like a glass marble filled with different opaque colors.

—Erin Ramos, effects animation supervisor

TOP LEFT **IKER DE LOS MOZOS ANTON (MODEL)** & **LISA KEENE** *Digital* | TOP RIGHT AND BOTTOM **BILL SCHWAB** *Digital*

LISA KEENE *Digital*

One challenge was figuring out how to light darkness. Not just emotional darkness but literal Water-Spirit-underwater-during-a-storm darkness. We started with some artwork that depicted bioluminescence. It was a sort of luminous energy that the Water Spirit has that only manifests when it's really active. We also used light sources that would occur naturally in the environment, like lightning. There are some shots that are so dark you don't see the horse—but then the lightning strikes and you see it. Both things really enhance the action and suspense of that sequence.

—Mohit Kallianpur, director of cinematography, lighting

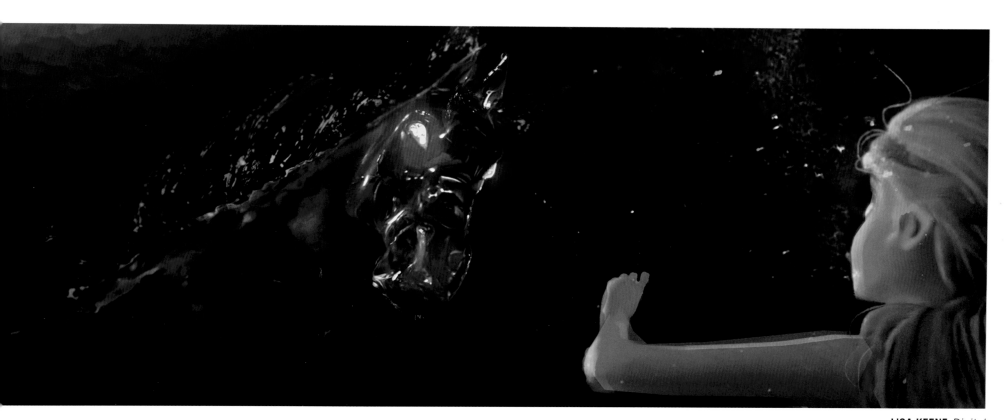

We explored different ideas for how to depict a horse made of water when it appears underwater: the cloudiness of ink in water, dark shapes over light, underwater volcanic steam vents where the heat of water adds some blurriness, the use of bioluminescence to create a magical glow. We make films with elements that are so fanciful, so we look for counterparts in the real world to help make those elements believable. It gives us inspiration for where to go and how to create something unique that no one's ever seen before.
—Dale Mayeda, head of effects, animation

ELSA'S MAGIC

Elsa's powers have grown. When she froze the fjord in the first film, the water was very placid and still. But in this film, she has to freeze the huge, crashing waves of the Dark Sea. As Ahtohallan calls to her, she channels memories and creates sculptures that she doesn't know the meaning of because she's not intentionally creating them. She's taking on aspects of nature that are much more powerful than she is and facing obstacles she hasn't had to face before. It's a very humbling experience for her.
—Steve Goldberg, visual effects supervisor

LISA KEENE *Digital*

LISA KEENE *Digital*

It was difficult to imagine drawing Elsa's powers in storyboards. We didn't want it to look like anything anyone had seen before. In the first film, we decided that her magic is an expression of her emotions. In this film, her emotions are evolving and maturing; that affects her powers, which are also growing. We had to determine how to depict that visually.
—Normand Lemay, head of story

LISA KEENE *Digital*

Elsa is freezing waves as they're in motion; the water is turning to ice and then crumbling; and she and the Water Spirit are interacting with the water. All of that introduced new technical challenges. We start with the tool sets we already have because we never know what they're capable of until the artists start playing with them. When the tools can't give the desired artistic effect, we partner with software engineers and technical directors to solve those challenges. There's a lot of input from art direction too, because whatever we build must achieve the particular look that the show is going for. For *Frozen 2*, we used a simulation engine that can handle a granular medium at different degrees of viscosity, like water, mud, and snow, and played with how to turn individual particles of water into a solid block of ice that still interacts with the water around it. There's a lot of hard work and collaboration—and then magic happens.

—Mark Hammel, technical supervisor

SEQ 250 SHAPE GUIDE FOR ICE STRUCTURES

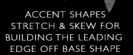

PUSH BEVELS FORWARD SHOWING
FORCE AND DIRECTIONALITY

ACCENT SHAPES
STRETCH & SKEW FOR
BUILDING THE LEADING
EDGE OFF BASE SHAPE

SIDES OFF BASE SHAPE CREATE A
TROUGH SHAPE THAT CUTS THROUGH
AND PUSHES AWAY THE WATER

SIDE-VIEW

SHOWING FORCE AND
DIRECTION, INTERIOR ACCENT
SHAPES CAN BREACH THE
BASE SHAPE SLIGHTLY

BASE SHAPE FRONT END
WITH ACCENT SHAPES

TOP VIEW

SEQ 250 SHAPE GUIDE FOR SLIDE STRUCTURES

ACCENT SHAPES FAN OUT FROM THE LEADING
EDGE FOR A CLEAR READ ON FORCE AND DIRECTION

SNOWFLAKES STAY STITCHED TOGETHER
WITH BASE ICE, CREATING A RUNWAY
TOWARDS ELSA'S "BIG WAVE" FREEZE

DAN LUND *Digital*

water line

Elsa's boat for Anna and Olaf

ABOVE **BRIAN KESINGER & LISA KEENE** *Digital* | ALL OTHERS **LISA KEENE** *Digital*

Elsa creates a boat-like vehicle for Anna and Olaf to float away in. A traditional boat didn't feel right, so we looked at sleighs because they have runners on the bottom, allowing them to scoot along the land for a while before hitting water. The shape reminded us of gravy boats, and we used that as the base shape. Since Elsa planned this vehicle, it's not "panic magic"; it's made out of thick, translucent ice embedded with snowflakes, like Waterford crystal. It's carrying people she loves, so she made it deep enough to cradle them and keep them safe. We always ask ourselves, What is this character thinking, why is this being made, and for what purpose? There's an emotional as well as practical logic to everything we design.

—Lisa Keene, co-production designer

Elsa's life raft

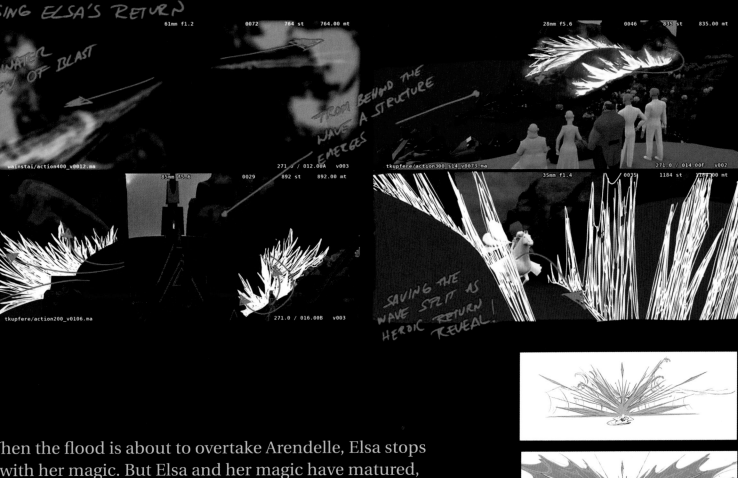

hen the flood is about to overtake Arendelle, Elsa stops
with her magic. But Elsa and her magic have matured,
rather than just erecting a barrier that then dissolves
e danger, she uses her magic to soothe the water. It's the
rst time she uses the unity symbol, which is her signature
nowflake but comprised of the elements, a combination
f the two. Elsa is the center that brings it all together in
armony. It's a climactic moment, but she uses her magic
a way that has a calming effect after the mayhem.

Dan Lund, effects animator

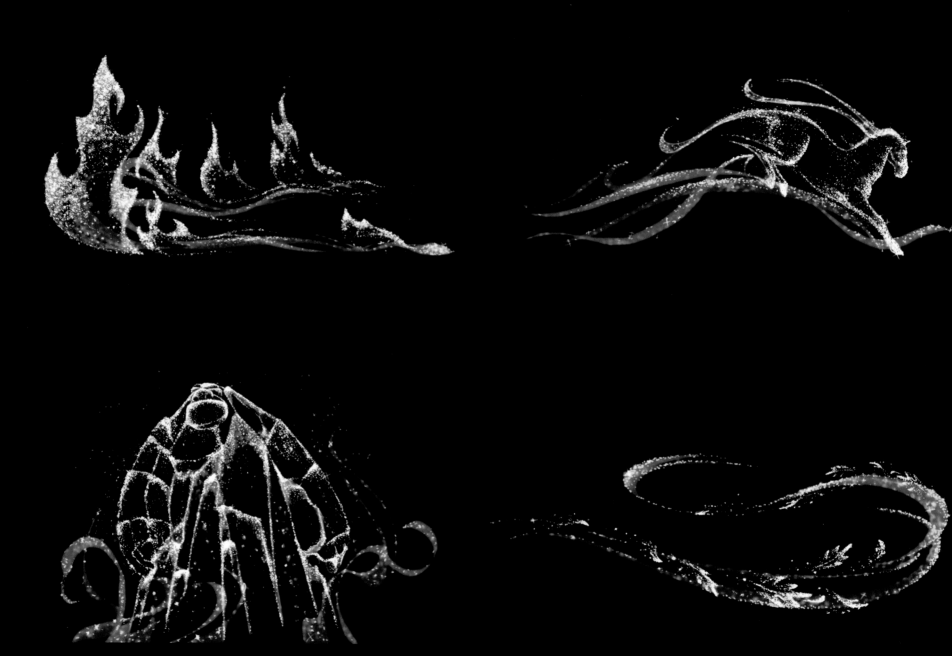

Into the Unknown Mist

LISA KEENE *Digital*

Elsa has used ice to create things that are quite beautiful, and she has used it to protect herself. Her ice looks very different for each situation; there's a language to it. For the sequence in which she harnesses the Water Spirit during a storm on the Dark Sea, we had to determine the language of her ice in an emergency when she doesn't have time to make it beautiful. For the bridle she creates for the Water Spirit while underwater, we referenced crystals and the way rock candy is strung on a string—fluid, fast, broken up—then wove that concept into the raft she creates so she won't drown. She's making ice in wind so there is a direction to it, like horizontal icicles. If you threw water into the air and the wind caught it, the first part of the water would hold some kind of shape for a moment, but the rest of it would *whoosh* off it as it blew away. To describe it to the team, I referenced a peanut butter and jelly sandwich, with the bread on the top and bottom and all the peanut butter—crunchy!—and jelly squished out of the middle.

—Lisa Keene, co-production designer

INTO THE UNKNOWN”

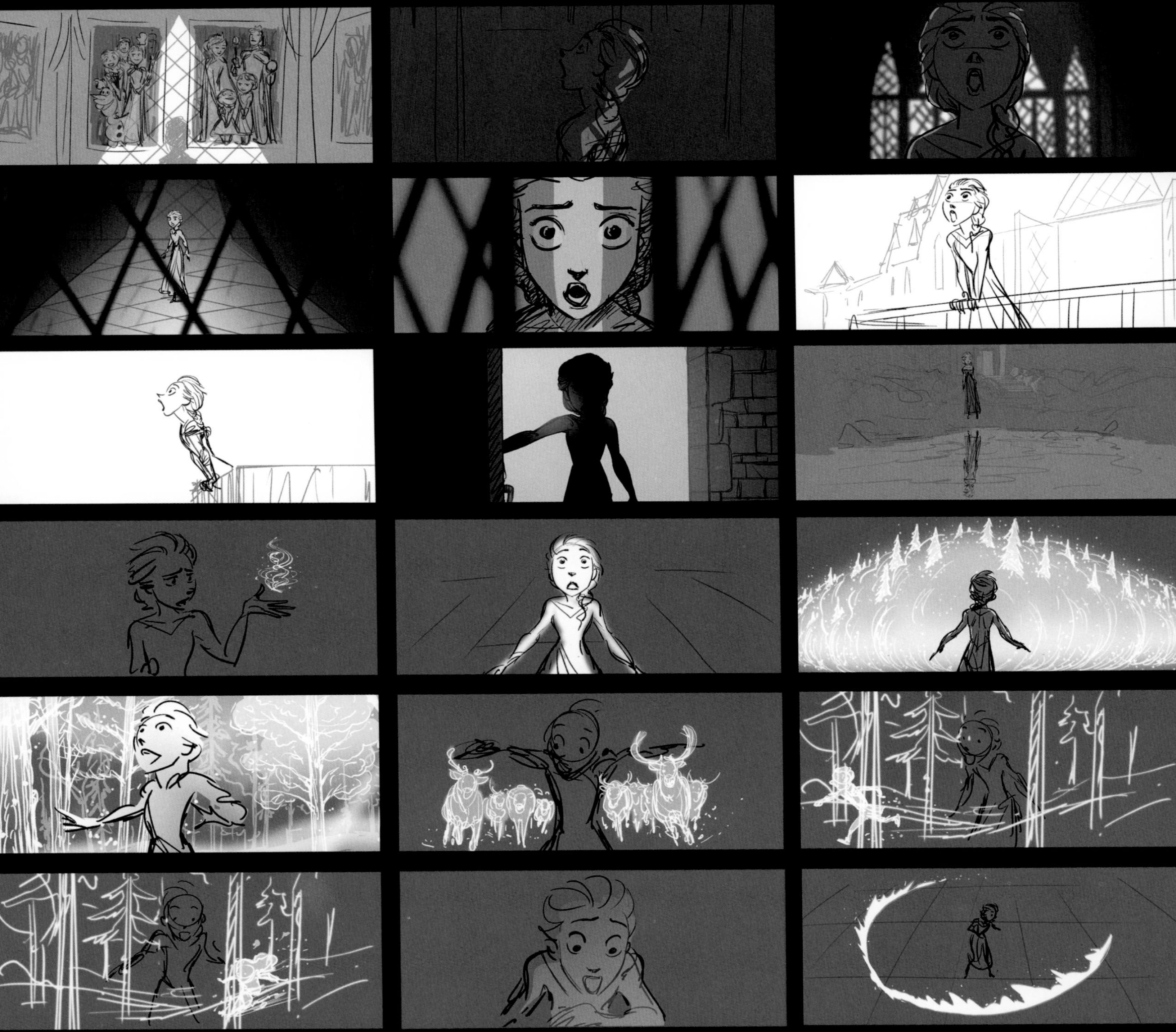

NORMAND LEMAY *Digital*

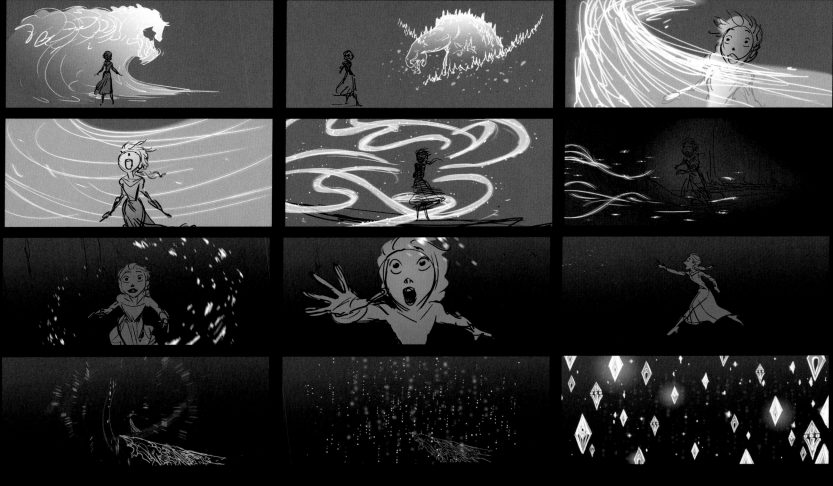

The song "Into the Unknown" is about the inner struggle Elsa is experiencing. She hears a voice she can't quite figure out. It's an abstract pull, the sense of a new chapter in one's life when you feel a change is coming, but you don't know what it is yet. She's feeling both apprehension and anticipation. It's deeper than something that's just stressful or exciting. Elsa knows everything she gained—reuniting with Anna, becoming queen of Arendelle—may be at risk if she gives in to the temptation of this voice. She wants to be content, but there's a gnawing feeling that she's not quite fulfilled. She tries to push it away, but she can't deny something is pulling her toward the unknown.
—Normand Lemay, head of story

DAVID WOMERSLEY *Digital*

AHTOHALLAN

Ahtohallan is both beautiful and menacing. The environment is made of ice and snow, and it is moving around as walls and passages shift for Elsa. Images form around her, and she has to know what the images are depicting, but they still have to look like they're made of ice and snow. The images are memories held inside Ahtohallan, so they are physically inside the glacier, not projected on its surface, and they're forming as Elsa is looking at them, not there waiting for her. It's a strange place that becomes welcoming and provides some answers, but Elsa goes too far.

—Marlon West, head of effects, animation

DAVID WOMERSLEY *Digital*

For Ahtohallan, we wanted to create an iconic silhouette. Glaciers are called rivers of ice, and this one flowed into a bowl-like shape with peaks surrounding it. The design challenge was creating a landscape that looked like the real world but that would also appear as Elsa's memories and experiences. We took scenes and locations that are familiar but made them more dream-like.

—David Womersley, art director, environments

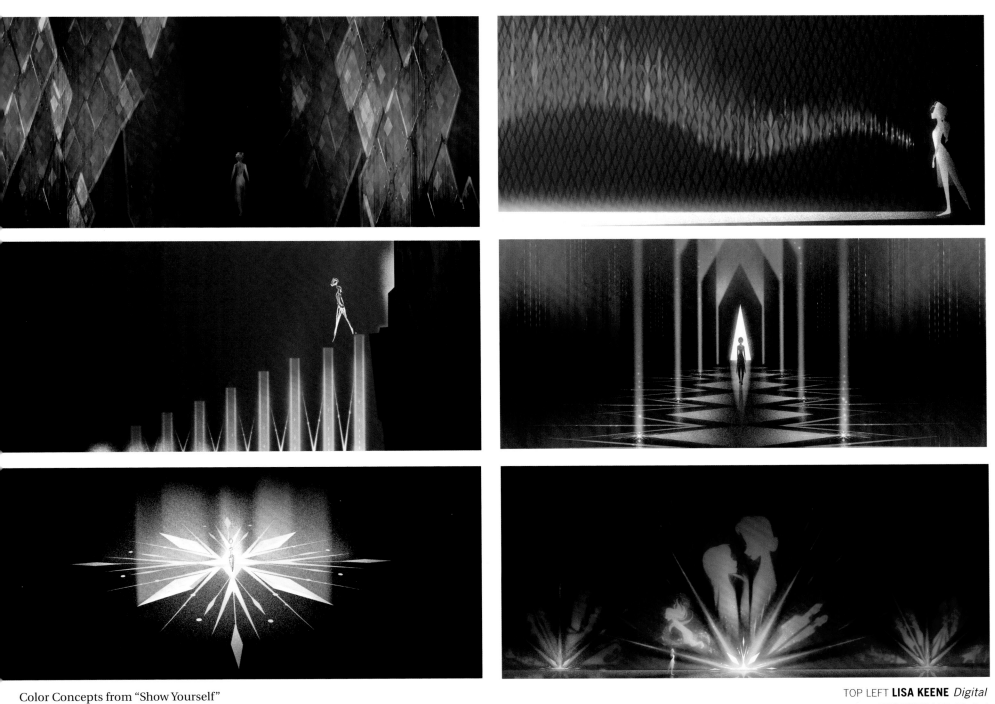

Color Concepts from "Show Yourself"

TOP LEFT **LISA KEENE** *Digital*
ALL OTHERS **BRITTNEY LEE** *Digital*

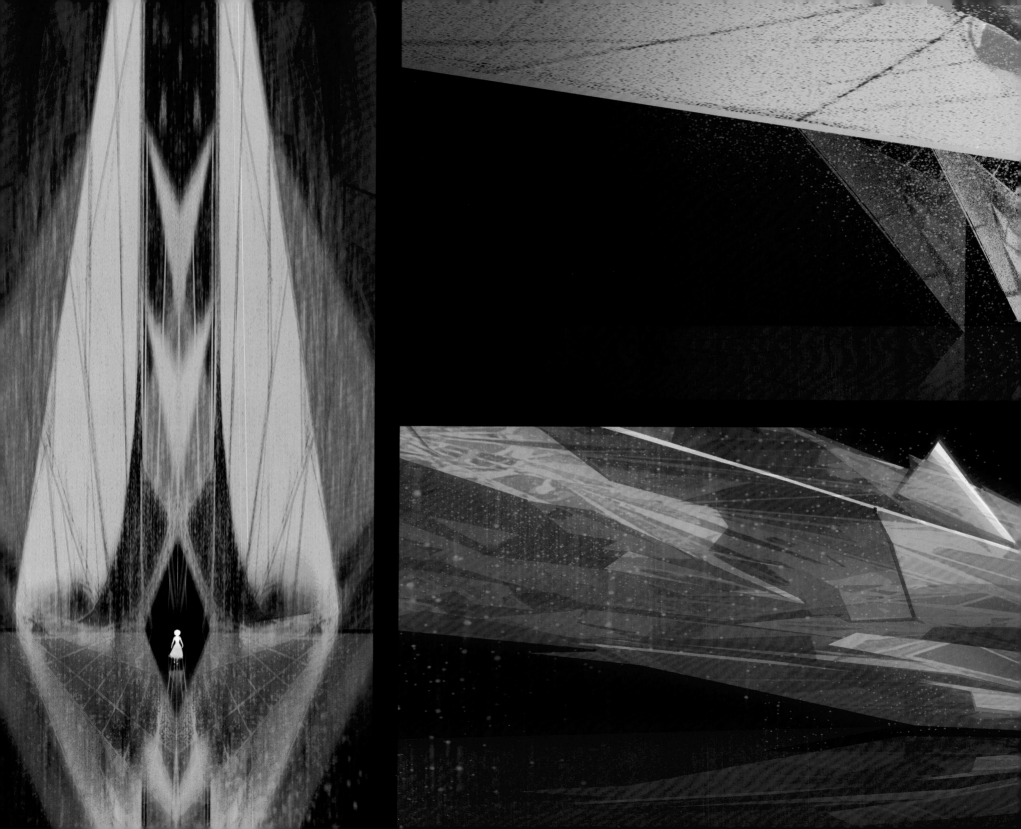

Ahtohallan is a cerebral, surreal place, yet it still had to have natural components. It was originally conceived of as an entirely organic structure like one would see in nature. It was later decided to add architectural features like the four elemental icons that beckon Elsa into Ahtohallan. Its final design combines properties of a glacier with highly theatrical characteristics.

—Michael Giaimo, production designer

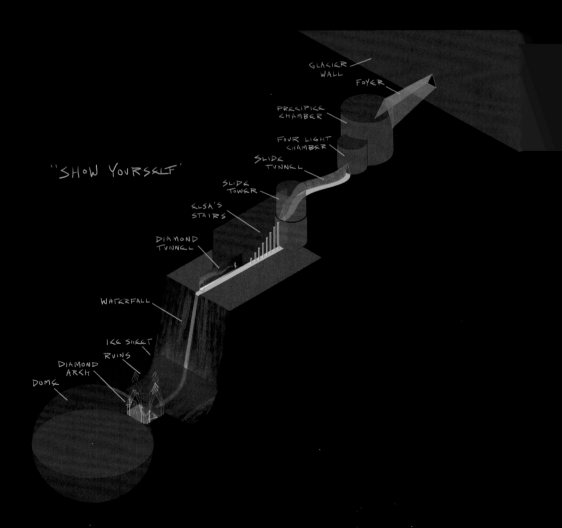

"SHOW YOURSELF"

GLACIER WALL

FOYER

PRECIPICE CHAMBER

FOUR LIGHT CHAMBER

SLIDE TUNNEL

SLIDE TOWER

ELSA'S STAIRS

DIAMOND TUNNEL

WATERFALL

ICE SHEET

RUINS

DIAMOND ARCH

DOME

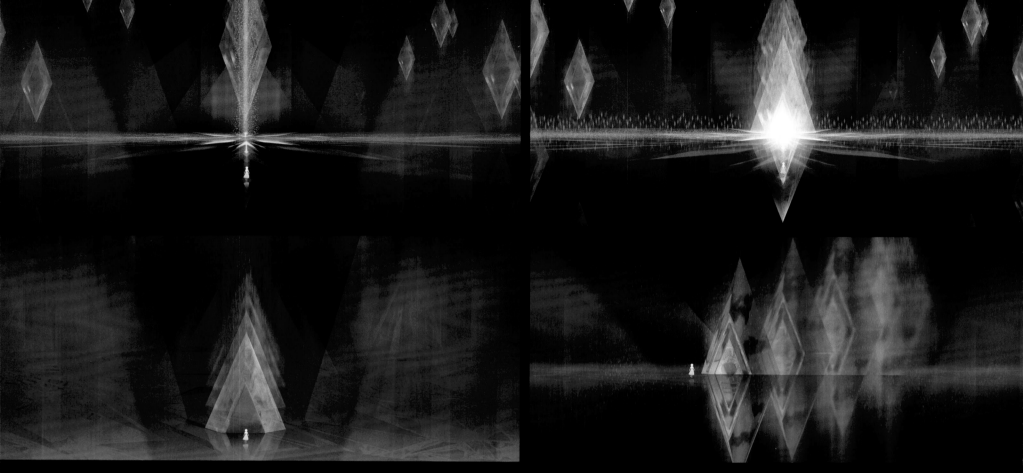

JUSTIN CRAM *Digital*

When the artistic and technical departments were asked to think about what Ahtohallan could be, everyone came up with wildly different responses. We referenced images of deep glacial ice, but that's not the same as what it would look like when someone is physically moving through it. And ultimately, there has to be a truth to materials for audiences to really believe in what's depicted on-screen. During the exploration phase, we discovered that across huge expanses of glacial ice, light is absorbed at different rates: Red is absorbed the fastest, then green, then blue. What that means is that deep glacial ice has a really rich aquamarine hue that gets refracted back through this clear ice that has an undulating surface.

COLOR SCRIPT

STORYBOARD

PAINTED KEY

100 Prologue	105 Iduna's Lullaby	107 Pumpkin Patch	112 Some Things Never Change	140 Into the Unknown
170 When I Am Older	170 When I Am Older	190 The Wind Spirit	205 Ice Has Memory	210 Meet the People	211 Hear the People Sing
245 River Pit	250 Dark Sea	250 Dark Sea	253 Elsa's Signal	255 Show Yourself	260 Snow Melt
273 The Forest Is Free	275 Reunion	285 Epilogue	285 Epilogue

LISA KEENE *Digital*

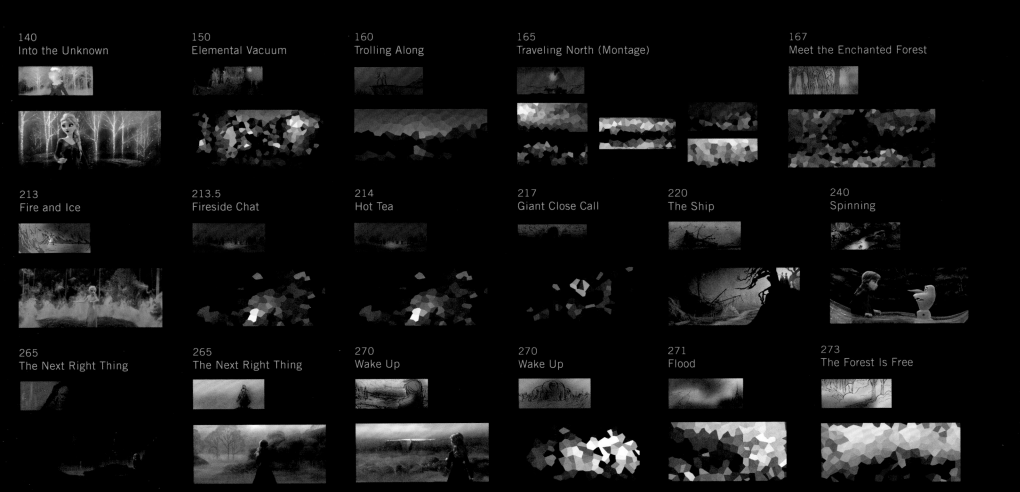

140
Into the Unknown

150
Elemental Vacuum

160
Trolling Along

165
Traveling North (Montage)

167
Meet the Enchanted Forest

213
Fire and Ice

213.5
Fireside Chat

214
Hot Tea

217
Giant Close Call

220
The Ship

240
Spinning

265
The Next Right Thing

265
The Next Right Thing

270
Wake Up

270
Wake Up

271
Flood

273
The Forest Is Free

The color script puts together narrative and art direction to depict the emotional arc of the film through color in key scenes. It usually starts with storyboards (top row of each line above) to determine a basic palette using foundational moments, then moves into painting (bottom row of each line above) as scenes become more specific and defined as the film progresses. Combining the cooler palette of *Frozen* with the autumn tones of *Frozen 2* was a challenge. We had to nod to the past while still speaking to the future. Overall, *Frozen 2*'s palette contains cooler reds and magentas, offset by neutrals, and we don't use a lot of yellows. That color appears mainly in the highest treetops for most of the film. But we break that rule in Arendelle. Allowing yellows in that space helps the audience to feel a real difference between fall in the village and fall in the forest. Arendelle has the most neutral tones. In contrast, the Enchanted Forest explodes with color.

—Lisa Keene, co-production designer

DAVID WOMERSLEY *Digital*

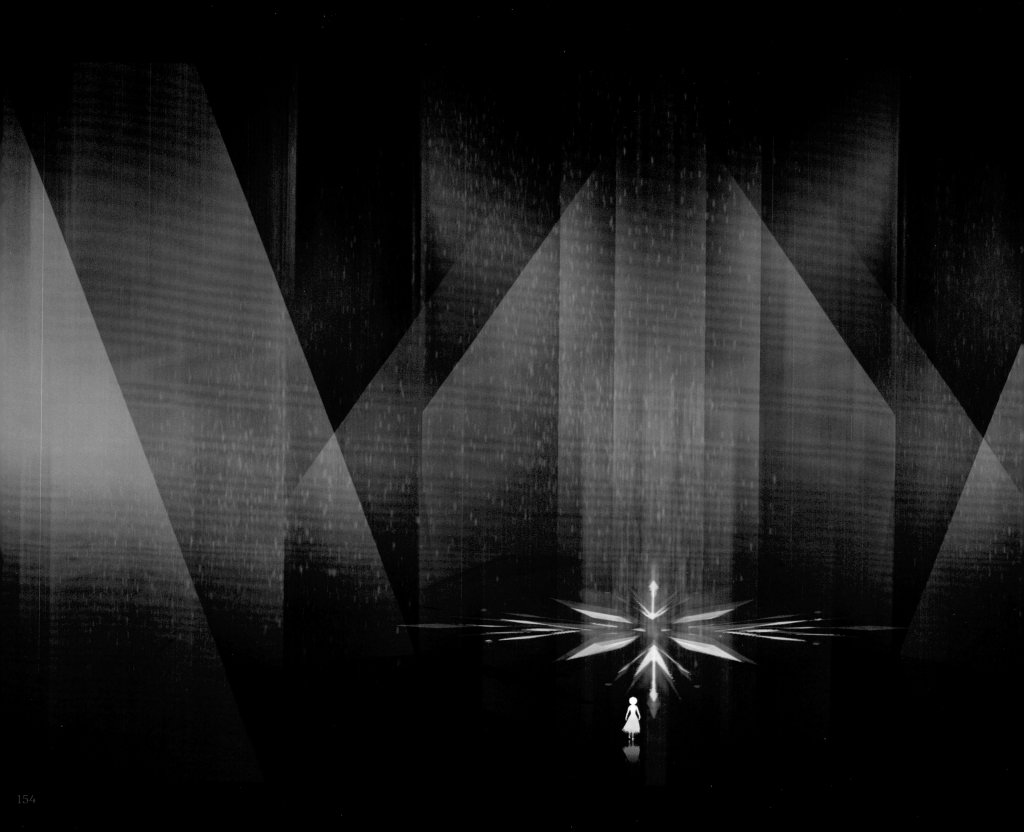

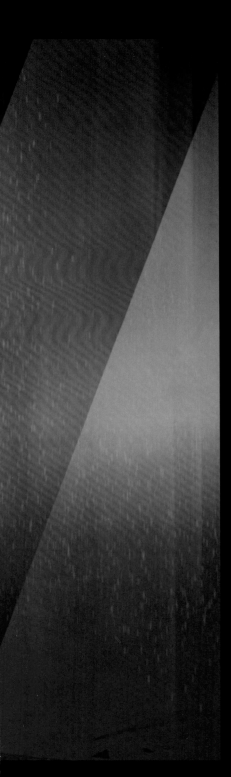

ACKNOWLEDGMENTS

I have a special place in my heart for *Frozen* and the filmmakers who created that beautiful film, so I am deeply honored to write this book celebrating the artistic creation of *Frozen 2*. Peter Del Vecho, Chris Buck, Jennifer Lee, and Michael Giaimo, thank you for trusting me to tell a small part of the story.

Thank you to Lisa Keene, David Womersley, Bill Schwab, and each incredible artist who took the time to share their creative thought process with me. You poured your heart, soul, and mind-boggling creative talent into this film, and it shows. The primary focus of this book is on the visual development that inspired much of the creativity and art that went into the final film. We tried to include work from other parts of the pipeline wherever possible, and we cannot express enough our gratitude to all the artists and production people who brought life to the final film. Lauren Brown, Nicole Buchholzer, Kelly Eisert, Nicholas Ellingsworth, Stephanie Lopez Morfin, Brandon Holmes, Kaliko Hurley, Brittany Kikuchi, and the entire *Frozen 2* production management team: Aside from the hard work you do to keep the production actually going, you are all just awesome people. Thank you so much for everything you do.

A special thank you to all of the wonderful people we met in Norway, Finland, and Iceland during our research trips throughout the years, including the Sámi people.

Alison Giordano, this book wouldn't have happened without you. Beth Weber, I am grateful for your patience and editorial guidance. Thank you to Toby Yoo and Pamela Geismar for designing and delivering a beautiful book. Kelly Kanavas and Michael Hebert, thank you for getting it all done and being the conscientious, wonderful people you are. Thank you to the development department of the Walt Disney Animation Studios. I am lucky to work with you every day.

Thank you to Mom for being my center of gravity, to Shannon for being my third ear, and to George for the joy.

JUSTIN CRAM *Digital*

LISA KEENE *Digital*

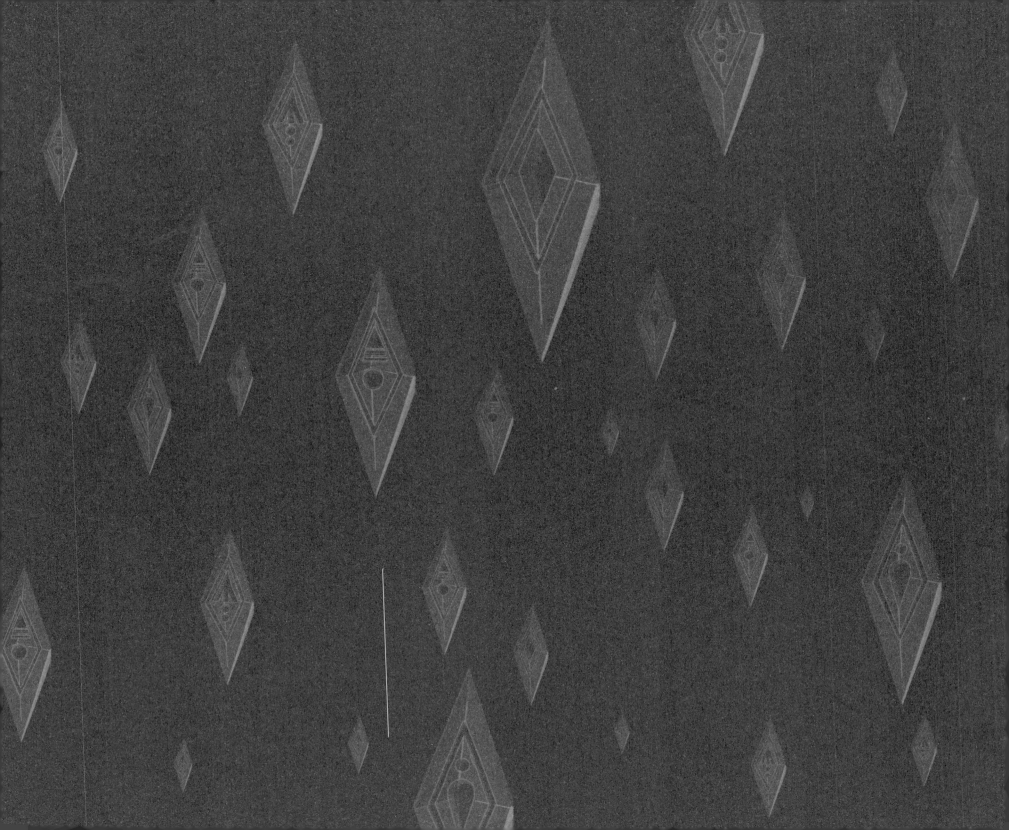